Her eyes wide in the moonlight, he brought his face down to the graceful curve of her neck and shoulder...

"You smell like such an angel," Neil said.

Kathy pushed him again, more forcefully this time. It wasn't him she was struggling against, it was her own warm, burning desire.

"No," she moaned and took a step back. Her heel lit on a clump of turf and she stumbled. He caught her up and brought his mouth back to hers, ruthlessly this time, plundering the silken treasure of her mouth. She'd never been kissed like this before...

Nothing in her experience had prepared her for a man like Neil Stratton!

Dear Reader:

After more than one year of publication, SECOND CHANCE AT LOVE has a lot to celebrate. Not only has it become firmly established as a major line of paperback romances, but response from our readers also continues to be warm and enthusiastic. Your letters keep pouring in—and we love receiving them. We're getting to know you—your likes and dislikes—and want to assure you that your contribution does make a difference.

As we work hard to offer you better and better SECOND CHANCE AT LOVE romances, we're especially gratified to hear that you, the reader, are rating us higher and higher. After all, our success depends on *you*. We're pleased that you enjoy our books and that you appreciate the extra effort our writers and staff put into them. Thanks for spreading the good word about SECOND CHANCE AT LOVE and for giving us your loyal support. Please keep your suggestions and comments coming!

With warm wishes,

Ellen Edwards

Ellen Edwards
SECOND CHANCE AT LOVE
The Berkley/Jove Publishing Group
200 Madison Avenue
New York, NY 10016

THE GOLDEN TOUCH
ROBIN JAMES

A
SECOND CHANCE AT LOVE
BOOK

Many thanks to
Danny, Blaine, Chuck, and Kathy.
And to Sue,
may her dented tubas
always tap out with ease.

THE GOLDEN TOUCH

1

KATHY ALLISON CARTER was locked in a staredown with a sousaphone. The sousaphone was winning. She thought of the sign she had hung so hopefully over the door of the little storefront two years ago: "Kathy Carter's Instrument Repair." Instrument Disrepair, she thought ruefully. The sousaphone was in worse shape from her attempts to repair it than it had been when it was brought in. Before it had been playable, though battered with dents. Now, John Philip Sousa himself couldn't have gotten a note out of it.

She knew she should have known better than to start on the sousaphone at this stage of her eroded patience. Today was Saturday, and it was spring in Apple Grove, Wisconsin. Outside of her shop, the golden sun was slanting long rays over the shower-dampened lilac bushes which grew in the median strip of Broad Street, sending up a heady scent and lavender sheen which competed with the brilliant pink of the flowering crabapple trees that grew on the grounds of the courthouse at the end of the street. But inside, Kathy was sitting back at her workbench, pondering the events which had led to her sitting inside on such a lovely spring day, at the age of twenty-four, wrestling with a brass band

1

instrument that had also, perhaps, seen better days.

It may have had something to do with her father being a minister; or maybe that meant she should have known better. But when Mr. Woods, the high school music director, had asked people to search their attics and basements for old instruments to donate to the community orchestra, it had been Kathy's own voice which had cheerfully piped up, volunteering to repair the instruments at cost, on her own time. But she hadn't been prepared for a flute twisted into the shape of a boomerang or a clarinet that had been carrying a peanut butter sandwich for twenty years. Saturday was normally the day she closed the shop, but here she was, working away, finally losing her sense of humor after crouching over her workbench for twelve straight hours.

Glaring into the sousaphone's bell, Kathy studied her reflection, which the flaring brass surface mischievously distorted in the manner of a fun-house mirror. Her small nose looked big and the blond hair knotted on top of her head trickled around her exaggeratedly tapered cheeks like squiggly snakes. And her nicely rounded chin had shrunk to nothing. Her neck, in the reflection, had disappeared completely into her buttoned-to-the-top Peter Pan collar, which was good, because to her it seemed too long anyway. The long legs, long arms, and long neck that looked so chic on the models in *Vogue* were—well—just plain excessive on herself. Lanky Kathy. She smiled, threw back her head, and said aloud, "Does anyone realize how noble I am? How selfless? How . . . hungry?"

Her stomach was empty. She had eaten a cup of blueberry yogurt that morning, but upstairs in her little apartment she was out of milk, out of bread, out of fruit, out of orange juice, out of everything. Every hour she'd half-decided to take a break and walk down to the supermarket before it closed, but she was on one of her work binges today. A vein throbbed in her head. Incipient headache.

Someone tapped on the glass of the shop's front window, and Kathy turned her head to see Marijo Johnson, one of her piano students, with sunlight finding the gold tones in her very red hair. Having attracted Kathy's attention, Marijo waved enthusiastically, plucked at her nylon windbreaker, and opened it to show her pistachio-green t-shirt, holding it out so Kathy could see the silk-screened picture of a rock star on it. Neil Stratton. It seemed like every other person under thirty in town had one. The guy must be making a fortune. Kathy mouthed the words "Very nice!" at Marijo and, satisfied, the teen-ager went away.

Kathy blinked twice to clear the haze in her tired vision and admired her shop. The grape ivy hanging in the corner needed trimming, but it looked tropically lush, and brightly colored posters hung on the wall advertising different musical instruments. There was a counter spray-painted white that she and her dad had hammered together, and on it a little cardboard display holding calendars and ticket order forms for the Milwaukee Symphony Orchestra. Her workbench, which she had bought at a farm auction along with her desk, was scattered with the tools of her trade, and a bulletin board hung on the wall by the door, the feature of her shop she liked the most. She allowed people to tack handwritten advertisements of items for sale and notices of meetings on it. And she had a music box on her desk, one she had had since she was a little girl, with bears on it.

It was time for five minutes' rest. It wouldn't do her any harm. As Kathy pushed the sousaphone away and leaned back to stretch and yawn, she saw red behind her closed eyelids. She hadn't had much sleep the night before—at one o'clock in the morning after the movie had let out a gang of kids had driven up and down Broad Street honking their horns. Maybe she would make the rest ten minutes.

She reached for the knob of her old gray plastic radio and turned it on. An ad blared out for Neil Stratton's concert at Nordic Valley, the nearby ski resort which doubled in summer as an outdoor concert arena, a natural amphitheater, which drew people from four states to its events. Him again. She had heard enough about that concert to last her a lifetime. Even her sister Renee was going. It was absurd that they were still advertising it. The tickets had sold out within twenty-four hours, but apparently the air time had been bought months in advance, so the station still ran the ads. The background to the announcer was a medley of Stratton's songs. When the ad was over, a different announcer said pompously, "We're sorry, the Neil Stratton concert has been sold out."

"No kidding, Sherlock Holmes," Kathy said aloud and changed the station resolutely to one featuring classical

music. Renee always did that when she was minding the
store for her—tuned in a rock station—and when Kathy
wanted to listen, she had to change it back. Her favorite
station was playing Offenbach, but for some reason Stratton's songs stayed in her mind.

It wasn't her kind of music really, but then, Neil Stratton
hadn't become popular by accident. His songs were lilting,
sensual, and his voice had a uniquely seductive rasp to it.
She had seen his picture everywhere; it seemed that when
the media latched onto a favorite star, they couldn't let go.
As a consequence, facts about him were well known even
to people like Kathy, who didn't normally follow the music
scene. He came from a rich family in Virginia—old
money—and had been a Fulbright scholar at the University
of Chicago. His songs scored high on pop charts, rock
charts, and country charts. His two movies had received
critical raves, and an Oscar nomination. He had won two
Grammy Awards. He was one of those people who seemed
to have been born lucky. It was enough to make you sick,
she thought, all that success. Must be nice.

She put her elbows on the table and rubbed her eyes.
Envy always flourishes on an empty stomach. Should she
go and lie down on the couch in the back room, or should
she take the walk to the store she had been postponing? Or
should she go back to the sousaphone?

Her decision-making was interrupted irritatingly by the
distinctive roar of a Harley-Davidson motorcycle on Broad
Street. It did her headache no good at all. She saw the
motorcycle flash by her window and then heard it revving
for a moment before it stopped down the street. Someone
thinks they're James Dean. What a royal pain in the neck.
Kathy rested her head in her hands.

She looked up when the door jingled. It was obviously
the rider of the motorcycle—evident from the brown leather
bomber jacket and the helmet with a smoke glass visor he
was pulling from his head. Oh, no. She knew it was just
one of those silly small-town prejudices, but for her mo-
torcyclists had a bad image based on old Marlon Brando
movies where small towns like Apple Grove were destroyed
by leather-jacketed hoodlums. He seemed to have a pack
slung on his back.

But if the man in the leather jacket had mayhem on his

mind, it was well hidden under the half-smile that was curving on his face. Heavens, what an attractive male. Specimens like that didn't make a habit of walking into "Kathy's Instrument Repair." Somewhere in the back of her mind, Kathy was surprised to feel a tiny synapse that meant that somehow she recognized him. Try as she would, she couldn't place the man. He was older than she—perhaps in his late twenties. Could he be one of her old friends from high school? Someone she'd been introduced to at summer camp? At college? Impossible. None of the possibilities rode motorcycles or wore leather. And the face before her was not one she would have forgotten readily.

He had nice features, though he wasn't what she'd call male-model, pose-for-perfume ads handsome. His face had too much character in it for that, and a glint of humor that hinted he didn't take himself too seriously. In a world filled with tension and pomposity, that quality was intently compelling. Dangerous. His hair was deep brown, full-bodied and shining. It was cleverly cut to a medium length so that it fell naturally and totally avoided the too scissored, too carefully arranged look that was so fashionable. Slightly disheveled from the helmet, it was already beginning to fall back into place.

His cheekbones were high and wide-set, his jaw firm, and there was a tiny scar on his cleft chin. There was nothing particularly remarkable about his build—it was just the right amount slim and gracefully put together, though his shoulders had a look of strength to them. Good grief, why was she thinking about his body?

Feeling embarrassed, she raised her eyes quickly to his. They were pale blue—but, oh, what a pale blue, with an inner brightness, a calm study to them that was focused, just now, on her face. Instantly, she was taken aback. The man looked as though he could read every thought that passed through her head. Kathy didn't often find herself at a loss with someone, but to her dismay, she felt rather intimidated. She hoped none of that showed on the surface. Her hand strayed self-consciously to the straggling curls on her forehead. She lowered it quickly. Shape up, Kathy girl.

He had let her study him with a certain cool and rather amused patience. In fact, it seemed disconcertingly as though he were accustomed to that kind of survey. Then, as if he sensed that she had completed her catalogue of his features, he lifted the shoulder strap over his head. In the silhouetting light from the window, she saw that he held a battered guitar.

"I've got a problem," he said. "Maybe you'll be able to help me?"

The words might be ordinary, but the man in front of Kathy had an extraordinary voice. It was one beat quicker than a drawl, and marked by a delicately sexual rasp that licked its way into her body through the spine. She watched him lay his guitar on the counter, his voice echoing through her like the memory of a caress. Good Lord! What made her think that? All at once it occurred to her that she couldn't remember what he'd said to her. The effect of his voice had been so intense that the content of his words escaped her.

"Please?" she said automatically, meaning "I beg your pardon?" It was a central Illinois usage Kathy had picked up in childhood from her mother.

"Please?" he repeated quizzically. Then, correctly interpreting an idiom that was obviously unfamiliar to him, he said, "Oh, I see. Can you replace a tuning peg?" The voice again, a warm handstroke on her heart.

He lifted the neck of the guitar and showed her the broken peg.

The way a parent responds to a youngster with a scraped knee was exactly the way Kathy responded to a damaged musical instrument. She stood up, too quickly, and at the same time realized who she'd just said "please" to. She'd seen his face on Marijo Johnson's chest. She'd heard his luxuriant voice on her old gray radio.

"Neil Stratton," she said. Black spots shot into her eyes, spots that turned red, then green. Retreating blood prickled in her fingertips, and a hundredweight of dizziness spread its rapidly intensifying pressure under her skull. Heartsick and humiliated, she thought, Oh God, why didn't I eat? I'm going to faint! And she did.

Which was how Kathy Allison Carter, small-town instrument-repair technician and piano teacher, happened to wake up in the arms of Neil Stratton, songwriter, musician, and celebrity of international repute.

Regaining consciousness was an unpleasant business that was like swimming to the surface of a heavily chlorinated pool after taking a belly flop from the high board. She was short of breath, her legs felt numb, and her eyes itched. Opening them with a few blinks, Kathy found she was lying on the old burgundy floral couch in her back room with Neil Stratton supporting her in one arm and gently applying a warm terry washcloth to her temples with the other.

"Could you drink a little?" asked the wonderful voice.

She nodded weakly. The hand with the washcloth left her face and returned in a moment with a paper cup, which was pressed lightly to her lower lip. Sipping the water, she became slowly more aware of his hard-muscled arm where it made warm contact with her back through the thin cotton of her shirt. He was so close she could feel his clean breath on her eyelashes and smell the spring breeze and leather from his collar, his hair.

After she'd fainted, he had obviously picked her up and brought her to the couch—and then what? The washcloth, the water—he must have found the washroom behind the stairs, looked in the linen closet for a washcloth, found the paper-cup dispenser behind the door. A man of resource.

"You know, I could see it if I were Elvis," he said. Kathy could hear the smile in his voice. "I don't get many swoons these days. It was charming, though, if a little old-fashioned."

Carefully, she was lowered to the couch and a lemon yellow bolster pillow slid forward to support her head. A sudden and unexpected pang of disappointment shook her as his arms withdrew from her body. Somehow, paradoxically, the most important thing in her life became to disabuse him of any notion that she had fainted because he was—well, who he was.

Mustering one's dignity is something of a challenge when one is spread flat out and disheveled on a couch, but Kathy did her best. Forcing herself, she looked straight up into the blue eyes that were studying her with such fine-honed perception. "I know how it must have looked, but it wasn't anything to do with you. I was hungry."

"You saw a hamburger on the floor and made a nose dive for it," he said, his tone too cheerfully agreeable.

Kathy tried again. "The only thing I've eaten all day was one cup of blueberry yogurt for breakfast."

He shook his head in mock condemnation. "When I saw

you, I thought—that looks like a girl who eats blueberry yogurt for breakfast." His finger traveled to her forehead and smoothed back the straying tendrils that had gathered there. "Hang on, alright? Don't try to stand up. I'll be right back."

He left her and in a moment Kathy heard the shop bell signal his departure. The air around her seemed still charged with his presence. The headache that had been threatening her all afternoon had disappeared. In its place had come a sweetly aching awareness in all the places on her body where he had touched her. Closing her eyes again, she flinched inside at the thought that she could be so vulnerable to a man, to his touch. It was a side of herself she had never dreamed existed, a hidden scar in her hard won independence. But then, Neil Stratton wasn't just any man. Perhaps she could be forgiven for a flash response to the magnetism that drew so many people into his fold. How suddenly life could rearrange its laws to resemble a crazy dream—except that this was not the kind of crazy dream she was prone toward. When he returned, she told herself sternly, there would be no more heart flutters over Neil Stratton.

Kathy was just getting around to wondering where he'd gone when she heard him return, turn the front lock, and flip the OPEN–CLOSED sign that hung on the shop door.

"Do you like turkey?" he asked her, displaying a sandwich wrapped in aluminum foil.

"But—isn't that your supper?"

"No. Sandy always packs too much."

Despising herself for being curious, determined not to let him see that she was wondering if Sandy was his latest lady love, Kathy let him put the sandwich in her hand. Then, as though he sensed her suppressed interest, and as though a natural courtesy demanded that he satisfy it, he said as she opened the foil, "Sandy's my bass player's wife. She likes to think that I need to be looked after."

If Kathy despised herself for being curious, she positively loathed herself for the intolerably irrational and stupid relief his words brought her. Surely the man could have a whole truckload of Sandys for all the difference it might make to her. She pressed open the foil.

"Wheat bread!" she exclaimed with involuntary dismay, and regretted the words instantly.

"Good for you," he said. Her criticism seemed to have displeased him not at all. In fact, he appeared to derive a certain sardonic amusement from it. Probably it confirmed some stereotype notion he had about her.

"I suppose," she said, "that I ought to be grateful it's not a vegetarian sandwich. Shredded seaweed, pâté of aloe vera..."

Good-naturedly, he picked up Kathy's wrist and carried her hand and his supper to her lips. "Never look a gift sandwich in the mouth, darlin'," he said, and settled his long body on the couch's armrest with easy-jointed grace. To her extreme discomfort, he sat there studying her while she ate, offering her the water cup at acutely knowledgeable intervals. Darn the man. What kind of empathetic power did he have over her that he could tell so exactly when she wanted a drink?

"Well," she said, after finishing, "I'm sorry now that I ate it. I ought to have saved it for posterity, it being *your* sandwich and everything."

"Don't worry," he said pointedly. "I'll autograph the crust."

Rude of him to mention how she hadn't eaten it. Straightening her back, brushing crumbs off her fingers, Kathy said coolly, "Well. It was nice of you to pick me up off the floor and feed me. Thanks a lot. I've kept you long enough. Shall we go and have a look at your guitar?"

"No," said Stratton, removing the foil that she'd been balancing on her knees. "I know you can't wait to reestablish the formalities and reassert yourself as a professional, but if you come bouncing out of that couch too quickly, you may end up on the floor again." He found the wastepaper basket, disposed of the tin foil, and came back to the couch. He cupped her shoulders in both hands and gently forced her to lie down. This time Kathy didn't bother denying to herself that she needed it, even though it was very likely that the swimming sensation in her head was caused by his touch.

"Masterful, aren't you?" she said resentfully.

He smiled. "Just take it easy. You don't have to worry. I closed your shop."

"I noticed," she said with a dry note in her voice. He immediately picked up on her discomfiture.

There was too much amusement in his voice as he said, "If being alone with me makes you nervous—"

"It doesn't!" she lied, trying to give him one of those blindingly confident smiles her older sister was so good at. It was hard to tell from his expression whether or not he believed her as he sat on the edge of the couch beside her. The movement brought his slim, warm thigh into contact with her hip, which he didn't seem to notice.

To cover her own embarrassment, Kathy said, "At least—was I graceful?"

"When you fainted? No. You fell over a tuba case and knocked over a bottle of valve oil. Mind you, my first thought was to call the rescue squad."

"Thank heavens you didn't!" she said with heartfelt gratitude. The town would have talked about it for weeks. "Anyway, we don't have a rescue squad, or a hospital or, for that matter, a doctor. When someone needs an ambulance, Carlton's Funeral Home sends the hearse and Mr. Carlton, the mortician, handles the emergency care while they drive the injured party to the hospital in Smithfield. Don't you have a concert to go to?"

"Yes," he said. "Later." Stratton's attentive, soft-eyed gaze wandered over her face and throat and then returned, with relentless precision, to her eyes. "Are you married?"

"No!" she said, startled.

"Do you have a boyfriend?"

"N–no."

"Then are you a nun?"

Getting angry: "No!"

"One never knows nowadays," he said with untouched serenity, as though he'd just asked her a reasonable question. "What am I doing that's making you so edgy?"

He sounded as though he really wanted to know, and yet there was an ever-so-subtle light in his eyes that warned her he'd already made a pretty accurate guess. Nor did she care for his choice of adjective. Edgy. The word had an intrusive subjectivity to it.

"Nothing at all," she said. "Though I'm not particularly accustomed to being scrutinized by celebrity superstars. Would you please not sit so close to me?" The tight contact of his thigh to hers eased obligingly as he moved back. A little more confidently, Kathy went on, "Why a motorcycle? Is your limousine in for a tune-up?"

"I don't have a limousine. While I'm on a concert tour, as now, a couple of semis and a bus haul my equipment and my—the people who travel with me—the road crew, their people, the band. Before I leave home, sometimes I throw the bike into one of the trucks. That way, whenever everyone on the tour gets sick of me—" he smiled—"I ride to the gig by the back roads. And I get some peace and the chance to experience the scenery."

Experience the scenery. What an odd way to put it.

"And bringing your guitar here was...?"

"An impulse," he answered. "I was riding by and your shop kind of smiled at me. Those yellow tulips in the window box. You know, this place has a warm look."

When the man decided to pay a compliment, he didn't kid around. The caress of his voice was so enticing that she could almost taste its honey in her throat. She had worked so hard to put sunshine into her little shop; it delighted her beyond measure when someone noticed it.

"Isn't that nice?" she said, sounding unnaturally bright. The flutter returned uninvited to her chest. "Your patronage is bound to be great for business. I can add to my sign— 'Where the stars bring their guitars.'" Her voice, that unconscionable traitor, cracked on the last word, and, pressing her fingers to her throat in embarrassment, Kathy discovered an open collar. It was her habit *always* to button her shirt all the way up. And here one...two...three...*four* buttons open! A blush began to climb the fair skin of her uncovered upper chest.

Observing her dismay, he said kindly, "In case you're wondering about it, I unbuttoned your shirt." His hands carefully stilled the fumbling movements of her fingers and, leaning slightly forward, he began to draw her shirt together and fasten the delicate silver buttons. "It was all in the line of duty. First-aid rule one: Lie the victim down and loosen restrictive clothing. And into that category, my friend, that collar of yours definitely fits. If you'd remained unconscious much longer, I would have had time to put my entire repertoire of anti-fainting techniques into practice. Mouth-to-mouth resuscitation, putting my head into your lap..."

A tiny gasp escaped her lips.

"Oh. Of course you're right," he said innocently, with hidden laughter and a tantalizing spice in his voice. "I meant to say, putting *your* head in your lap."

Instead of leaving her, his fingers stroked lightly over her collarbone, softly testing her flushed skin before his hands came to rest against the burgundy couch on either side of her head. His light gaze had become neither cruel nor threatening, yet it seemed to hold her captive to his will.

"Kathy." His voice was a rough, seductive whisper. "Don't be afraid of me."

His body was above her, close enough for her to share his fluid warmth, but not touching. His fragrance bathed her, the fresh minty tang of back country Wisconsin, where every spring leaf, every wildflower breathes out the secret perfume of a life cycle renewed and rich. As his mouth came to hers, she felt the soft mating of their breath before his lips found and opened gently over hers. Lower in her body surprised flesh pulsed to life and she closed her eyes against an overwhelming wash of voluptuous sensation.

Her shoulders were so filled with tension that they began to hurt her and the pain brought small shivers in its wake. He seemed to sense it immediately and his pliant fingers moved to caress her shoulders with practiced sensuality.

"Better?" he asked softly.

There was no free breath in her lungs to answer him, because her pounding blood was consuming it so swiftly. She sensed the luxury of his smile as he rested his fingertips on her cheek. And then he slid them lower to hold her chin between his thumb and forefinger before he kissed her again, more deeply, exploring her feminine mouth in a kiss that was expertly tentative, as his hands moved under her shoulders, molding her to him.

Kathy had to summon every last shred of her sapped will to duck under his arm, to stand, to turn and face him. No man had kissed her since—David . . .

The feelings she had blocked inside herself for years came blaring back to her in a sudden reminder. She had convinced herself she didn't need any of that, and was dismayed, even horrified, by the depth of her response to him, the deep timbre of her physical need. And worse, his blue eyes were taking her in, analyzing her astonishment and her anger.

"So, Mr. Stratton," she snapped, "am I to be another notch on your guitar case? It's so easy for you, isn't it?"

He stood. His smile was friendly, slightly ironical. "Apparently you don't kiss on the first faint."

"And how did you know my name?"

"It's emblazoned over your door in curlicued, baroque lettering, remember? No, I'm not making fun of it, so don't get excited about that, too. Look, I'm sorry if I made you mad at me, but you're a beautiful woman and I'll be damned if I'll apologize for kissing you."

Clutching tightly to her little remaining dignity, she turned, marched to the counter, and picked up his guitar. "What seems to be the trouble with your guitar, Mr. Stratton?"

He walked lazily to the other side of the counter and leaned over it gracefully, his expressive blue eyes sparkling. "Tuning peg," he said, touching it with a long finger.

"Ah, yes, of course; I saw that immediately." She studied the damage and looked back at him. "If this is the guitar you're planning to use tonight at your concert—"

"It isn't."

"Well, you happen to be in luck. I *can* fix it; but it's going to cost you."

"How much?" he asked.

"Fifty cents."

"I think I can handle it."

She carried it to the workbench and laid it down on her work space of carpet remnants covered with white sheeting. "I don't do much with guitars," she said. "Usually I send them out. But I keep a few tuning pegs around so I can fix the guitars the kids bring in, and they're made especially for cheap guitars like this one."

He smiled. "It's my second guitar; I've had it since I was thirteen. Sentimental value."

Darn that voice, she thought. He was way across the room, but she had the strong feeling that his arms were sliding around her. An intense desire to swallow betrayed her emotional state. He watched her take her tiny screwdriver out and begin to work, and then strolled around the counter to look at the sousaphone; he picked it up, the long artist's fingers working the mother-of-pearl keys.

"What's wrong with it?" he said.

"Don't talk to me about that stupid thing," she said. "It ate my dent ball."

"Your dent ball? Tell me about it," he said with seductive sympathy.

She sighed, pulling at a tiny screw with her fingernail. "You put a dent ball in, and work it down until it's under the dent, and then you tap on the outside with a plastic hammer until the dent comes up."

"Like an auto body repair."

"Precisely. But sometimes, the dent ball gets stuck." She tightened the tiny screw, and turned around to hand him the guitar. He had the sousaphone upside down and was shaking it, and with a metallic clatter, the errant dent ball rolled out into his hand. He shrugged and smiled, laying the horn and the ball on the counter, and took the guitar from her. She glared at the sousaphone with a look so fierce that icicles should have grown on it. She had suspected all along that it was male.

"That will be fifty cents, please," she said, turning back to him.

With a smile that pretended to be rueful, he took from his shirt pocket a credit card, and handed it to her, held sideways between two fingers.

"You don't carry cash?" she snapped.

"Sorry, no; you're welcome to pat down my hip pockets if you don't believe me."

Determined not to let him get the best of her, she bent down, pulled her little ticket maker from under the counter, set the card in the bracket, drew the bar across, press-copied the charge plate, and then with great deliberation, wrote out "One tuning peg, fifty cents, plus tax, fifty-two cents," and said, "Your signature, please."

He signed for her, using the pen that hung from a nail on the side of the counter. Neil Stratton, in big, bold letters that looked like an autograph. She tore off the carbon and handed him the copy.

"Will you come with me to my concert?" he asked.

She had been putting the ticket machine back, and almost dropped it at his words. "Wh-what?"

"Will you come with me to my concert?" he repeated patiently.

"I—I—me?" Sanity returned. "Of course not. Look, Mr. Stratton, I don't know what I've done to give you the impression that I'm the kind of girl who kisses on couches or goes to rock concerts, but I'm not. And I don't ride motorcycles either. If you make one slow circuit up and down Broad Street, you'll find so many people to sit on that motorcycle with you that it won't even move. What are you staring at?"

"Your lips," he said. "What are you doing later on?"

"What am I doing later on? An alto clarinet, a baritone bugle, and two solid nickel-silver French horns."

"Good," he said, and reached out to touch her cheek. "I'll see you then, Kathy."

She stood, rooted in place, while the bell jingled, while the motorcycle engine coughed into life. It had faded into the distance by the time she was able to move. Her breath was gone; she felt the way she had heard people did when they were having a heart attack. This was an emergency. She reached for the phone and dialed the four digits of her sister's number with shaking fingers. Renee answered after three rings, with her sunny, "Hel-lo!"

"Renee?"

"Kath, hi! Whatcha been up to, sweetie?"

"Neil Stratton was just here."

"What? Kathy, what's the matter with you? Speak up! What are you talking about?"

"Neil Stratton unbuttoned my blouse. I ate his sandwich and he kissed me."

"Kathy, you just stay right there, honey. I'll be right over." Kathy heard Renee calling to her husband. "Jack? Jack, where's the car keys? Watch the kids. I've got to get down to the shop. I don't know what happened, but I think Kathy's flipped her wig."

2

RENEE HAD TAKEN her in hand. They sat in the beer garden
at Tony's, the tavern at the far end of Broad Street. The
low sun gave the air a rose tinge. The tall yellow daffodils
nodded from their sentry positions in the freshly cut beds
outside the white picket fence, and the red brick of the plaza
surface felt warm under their feet. The red maple in the
corner was coming delicately into leaf, shimmering in the
late afternoon breeze. The garden was nearly empty. It was
suppertime and they had their pick of tables.

Renee sat across the round redwood table from Kathy,
her tongue in her cheek, her normally smooth forehead
wrinkled with concern, looking at Kathy over the purple-
tinted prescription sunglasses which were perched on the
end of her tiny nose. Her shoulder-length hair, finer and
straighter than Kathy's, with a glittery, touch-me look to
it, was parted down the middle and pulled back on one side
with a mauve comb, to reveal a perfectly shaped ear dec-
orated with a diamond stud. She was dressed for the concert
in a tightly cut mauve angora sweater and tight silk pants
with tapered ankles.

She had been the big sister, attractive, vivacious, had

17

led all the boys in town around with rings in their noses, and had finally culled Jack Olds, the farm-implement manufacturer's son, from the panting mob. And thus she had been catapulted in a small way from penny-pinching minister's daughter to vacations in Hawaii, designer clothes, and the big white Cadillac with onboard computer that sat on the gravel road under the oak tree across the sidewalk. In spite of their differing lifestyles, the two sisters were close.

"You need a drink, Kath," Renee was saying. "White wine," she said to Tony, who was hovering nearby in his white apron. He brought a glass for each of them on a painted tray.

"This is great," said Kathy. "Everyone who goes by will see Reverend Lawson's two daughters drinking before the sun is down."

Renee smiled at the idea. "Do you see anyone? Tony won't tell. Now, let's go through this again. And if this is a practical joke, because you know that Jack and I are Neil Stratton fans, I won't forgive you for at least—two days."

"Have you ever known me to make a practical joke?" Kathy asked.

"We have to be systematic. First, I want a positive identification of the culprit." She took a new copy of *Them* magazine from her black leather shoulder bag, thumbed through it, folded it back, and laid it on the table in front of Kathy. "Have you seen this face before?" she asked tersely.

Kathy put her fingertips on the edge of the magazine to keep the pages from blowing. The eyes looked piercing even in black and white, and he looked at the camera with his humorous half-smile. He had his arm around the brunette costar of his recent movie, and she was looking up at him and laughing as though he had just told the funniest joke in the world.

"Yes, that's him," she said. "That's the one." She felt strange, and flipped the page over. On the next page was a picture of him performing, backlit by a stage light, taken from such an angle that the picture showed his audience gazing up at him in rapt attention. And then there was a final picture of him standing beside his motorcycle. "That's the motorcycle," Kathy said. "He looked just like that." She took a small sip of wine and made a face. "The whole experience was like being run over by a truck."

Renee leaned back and swirled the wine in her glass. "Did you like him?"

"No," was Kathy's emphatic answer. "He was arrogant, conceited—and he got my dent ball out of the sousaphone."

"Would you please stop thinking for a minute about those stupid musical instruments of yours? I'll rephrase my question from 'did you like him' to—how did you feel about him?"

Kathy held her hands palms out in a helpless gesture.

"Do you think," said Renee softly, "that the reason this has upset you so much is not because it was the famous Neil Stratton, but because you were kissed by an attractive stranger?" Kathy had no reply. "Kathy, David's been gone more than a year."

"I know," she said quietly. "Renee, he asked me to go with him to his concert."

"And you turned him down? Oh, Kathy. You're crazy, Kathy. You've grown so used to saying no, you've forgotten how to say yes."

"Look, I might have gone if he'd just been going to any old concert, if he hadn't been who he was, you know? But you see, Renee—what would a man like that want with someone like me?"

"Well, what is this line now? 'If he likes me, there must be something wrong with him?' What's happening to you? You had healthier attitudes than that when you were thirteen."

"Renee, all he wanted was—well—like a little Wisconsin sticker on his suitcase. I met his criteria for a one-nighter: I'm a hick, I was prone, he was in the mood. What could be more convenient?"

"Sounds great to me," said Renee. "What could be more convenient, indeed? I can't understand you, Kathy."

"Oh, Renee, why don't you talk like a minister's daughter for once?"

But Renee wasn't about to. She slanted her eyes mischievously. "Was he a good kisser? Look at you blushing. He must have been wonderful."

"No, I'm not, I'm not blushing!" said Kathy, slapping her traitorous cheeks with both hands.

"And your eyes are glowing. What did that man do to you? He must have the golden touch!"

The color faded from Kathy's face into a look that was nearly fright. She picked up her wine glass, rolling it between her hands.

"Kathy, what's the matter?"

"It was—so sudden. Like a—reawakening. Like new blood in atrophied tissue." Kathy smiled ruefully.

"Do you think you'll see him again?" Renee was a little worried.

Kathy laughed and rolled her eyes. "Sure. On the next cover of *Time*. Other than that, not in two million years."

The announcer on the classical station said in his sonorous tones, "Ladies and gentlemen, it's twelve midnight. For those of you still listening, we'll play something lively in honor of the new day, the 1812 Overture." Kathy smiled in anticipation and turned the radio up even more, as far as it would go, so loud it drowned out the unusually noisy traffic on Broad Street, the cars, motorcycles, and souped-up vans returning from Nordic Valley.

The two-hour nap, the rubdown she had given herself with the cut lemon half on her skin and scalp, and the shower following had restored her to full bloom. She had towel-dried her hair, leaving it loose and curling on her shoulders, and snuggled into a dark grape pullover in a soft, loopy knit of lamb's wool and a pair of plush corduroy tailored slacks.

At ten-thirty Tony had come over from the beer garden, as he often did when he saw by the bright shop light that she was working late. Kathy had become Tony's pet challenge. His ambition was to create the perfect drink for a non-drinker, and Kathy was the perfect non-drinker. In Kathy, a tendency toward conservative personal habits, a strict religious upbringing, and a natural dislike for the taste of alcohol had combined to make her a dedicated teetotaler. Usually, when he arrived with his frothy concoctions so temptingly garnished with marischino cherries and orange twists, Kathy laughed, took a sip, made a face, and sent it back. But tonight Tony had brought a frosty quart glass brimming with a drink he called the "one-step, two-step, fall-over." She had taken a taste—fruit juice. He had denied it vehemently, and left with a slyly triumphant smile, warning her to sip it slowly. Laughing again, she had saluted him with the glass. What a tease he was! If there was alcohol in here, she'd eat an oboe swab.

Every so often she thought of how Neil Stratton had intimated that he'd come back after the concert, and it made her tense all over. Once she'd had the panicked feeling that maybe she should go to Renee's house, send the babysitter home, and spend the night there. Then she had thought the incident through again. She decided that his statement, "I'll be back," was only a nicer way of saying goodbye, because, after all, he had kissed her. What could he say? "Thanks for the kiss, guess I'll never see you again?" She thought of Renee sitting out at Nordic Valley watching him, devouring him with her eyes most probably, and thinking about his contact with Kathy. What would Jack say about it all? Probably his usual, "Damn, I wish that girl would meet someone and get married, and stop clinging to that dead boy's ghost."

By midnight the lingering feelings of sadness and tension had evaporated. Kathy was feeling pretty good. As a matter of fact, she felt splendid. Taking another refreshing gulp of Tony's fruit punch, she surveyed the last of her work. She had saved the gluing on of all corks to do at one time. The ventilation in her shop was poor, and the odors of the cements and solvents she used to fasten on corks could become a little overpowering. The labels advised the user that the company was not responsible for the ccnsequences to anyone who abused the product by concentrating and inhaling the glue vapors. Who would want to do a thing like that? Mind, the smell was becoming increasingly pleasant to her as midnight approached. A feeling of intense content tickled her. She giggled and swallowed more fruit punch.

"Boom!" went the first explosion of the 1812 Overture. She had been humming along loudly, and the *boom* almost made her fall off her stool. From then on, when the roar of cannons interrupted the music, Kathy pretended to have been shot, clutching at her chest and then her throat exuberantly, and gurgling "Aaaughh!" in mock agony. She lifted her glass and downed the last of Tony's concoction, saying "Boom!" and starting her stool in a giddy whirl.

Neil Stratton was leaning on the counter, chin in hand, watching her relaxedly.

"Oh, my God!" she said. Her startled hand hit and over-turned a box of bottom-action trumpet springs, and sent them springing all over the floor. "Oh no!" The last piece of crushed ice from the drink slid into her windpipe, and she began to cough and splutter.

Quickly, he came around the counter, took her arm, and rubbed her back. The small chunk finally dislodged and she tried to spit it up graciously into her palm.

"There," he said. "I'm very good with ice and dent balls. I'm also ready with the Heimlich maneuver."

Regarding him indignantly through steaming eyes, she said, "I'm sure you know all sorts of maneuvers. You almost scared me out of my few wits!"

He had changed his clothes to a blue turtleneck sweater beneath the leather jacket and western jeans fitted to his trim body. He reached over and turned off the radio, leaving the room strangely quiet, and picked up one of her hands. "I'm sorry I scared you, but I did say I was going to come back." A thrill was shooting up her arm at the sinewy touch of his musician's fingers.

With a curious smile hovering over his sensual lips, he lifted her tumbler and tasted what was in the bottom. "Te-quila."

Frowning, she said with majestic benevolence, "You're *quite* mistaken. It's fruit punch." But then, distracted by the sudden humor of the whole world, she dug her head into his shoulder and collapsed against him in giggles. "Did you see those springs? Did you see them? It was the funniest thing I ever saw! They were jumping all over the place like—like—"she was overcome with laughter—"like a bunch of little teeny men on pogo sticks!"

Laughing like she was, he picked up the bottle of glue, read the label, set it back down, and held her chortling frame at arm's length, studying her. She studied him back, with the gregarious and invincibly trusting smile of an infant.

"Lady," he said, "you're higher than Mount McKinley. How long have you been in here sniffing this stuff?"

Next to the springs, his question was the second funniest thing. "I haven't been sniffing it—I've been gluing corks! Honestly. I can't help it. I can't afford a vent fan. Do you know what they cost nowadays? I'll tell you what, though.

You send me all your guitars whenever they need tuning pegs and by the year 3000 A.D. I'll have enough money for one." She was giggling again.

"Higher than Everest," he said. "Do you have a jacket around somewhere?"

"Yes, I do, up in my bedroom." She pointed at him. "Ha! *That* was the Heimlich maneuver."

She could see that his eyes were full of laughter as he turned and disappeared up the stairs that led from the back hall. She knelt and tried to pick up the springs—no easy task. He returned carrying her fisherman's sweater as she was trying to stuff a handful of springs back into their box, with little success.

"Lively little things, aren't they?" she said.

"Come here, you," he said, laughing huskily and capturing her waist. "Lift your arms." He pulled the sweater over her head.

"Are you kidnapping me, Mr. Stratton?" she asked as her head came poking through the bulk of the sweater.

"Higher," he said, "than the space shuttle. Where's the key to the shop? Dr. Stratton prescribes an immediate dose of fresh air."

She danced over to the spot where she kept the key, and dangled it before his face. *"Voilà!"* she said, "On the hook by the door. *Sur le porte. Sur la porte?* Do you know that in high school I became so proficient in French that—ugh!" Propelled outside by his steady arm, she received the soft night air in the face like a benign slap. Behind her she heard him snap off the light, lock the door, and pocket the key.

There was a moment's vague paranoia that someone in one of the cars still going by on the street might see her with him, and that she would have to spend the rest of her life explaining what in the world she was doing getting into a car at midnight with an internationally known singer of rakish repute. Before she knew it, however, she was sitting in a sleek red Mercedes, with Neil Stratton fastening her seatbelt securely.

"You're a responsible soul, Mr. Stratton."

"Only when it suits me, Miss Carter." He started the car. "Where to?"

"That way," she said, pointing vaguely. "Where's what you were on earlier?"

"The bike?"

"Do you know what?" she said as he slipped the transmission into gear. "You've got to quit calling it a bike. *I* ride a bike. It has two things you pedal, a thumb bell that goes ting-a-ling, and brakes that fail when you're going downhill on wet days. What you were riding, Mr. Stratton, was *not* a bike. I thought we were going to ride motorcycles and I was going to be your moll, or your chick, or—what do you call them?"

Grinning, he said, "Women who ride motorcycles."

Kathy leaned back in the plush seat. "You're a square, Mr. Stratton."

One of his hands left the wheel just for a moment and gently tweaked one of her curls. "I thought you didn't like the bi–motorcycle, so it went back in the truck."

"And you bought a car just for me," she chirped.

"I *borrowed* a car just for you."

Hazily interested, she said, "From who?"

"I'm not sure. Someone else arranged it. Would you like your window down?"

A fresh breeze, sweetly seasoned with new green, touched her face as she watched the speedometer climb to thirty. He was going in the direction she had pointed, down a side street, the narrow way across town. In half a minute they were in an open stretch of farmland. The speedometer climbed to forty-five and stayed there. The headlights sliced into corners and reflected from the yellow plastic squares set in the center line. Hanging low in the sky was a big Wisconsin moon that was almost too big to look at.

"Is there anywhere you'd like to go?" he asked.

Anywhere that they wouldn't be seen. "Would you like to go to the Black Bridge?"

"I'm game," he said. "Where is it?"

"Follow this road to the barn with the Holstein painted on it and make a right." They went down a long hill and up another. The barn loomed at the top. He slowed and turned into a gravel road, and the tires spewed out little rocks.

"My sister and I always sing when we ride on gravel roads. It makes your voice sound funny. Want me to sing?"

"I would love to hear you sing. What do you know?"

"*Camelot,*" she said. "I know every word on the album.

And I've seen the movie seven times." She began singing, "Camelot! Camelot! I know it sounds a bit bizarre, but in Camelot... Oh, make a left after the next bend."

He pulled off the road into a rutted cowpath between an open wire fence. The engine purred to a stop.

The Black Bridge was one of Kathy's favorite spots. She opened her door without waiting for him, and ran down the path to the right-of-way and followed the tracks. She hadn't been here since the dead of winter. Then it had been simply, dramatically, white snow piled against black steel, with no sound but the keening of the icy wind. Now, the spring frogs were peeping, and the water from the Little Hawk River gurgled on the rocks underneath, and there was a lovely scent of new-tilled earth in the air. She walked out over the thick, evenly spaced creosoted beams and balanced on the rails, steadying herself on the iron side, feeling the thrill of being suspended in air. It was such a safe way to get that feeling, too—the spaces between the beams were only three inches wide. She heard him come up behind her.

"It really is a bridge," he said with a note of amusement in his voice.

"Of course it's a bridge. What did you think it was?"

"Oh, restaurant, supper club, barn dance—"

"Are you still feeling responsible? What do you make of this?" She flopped on her back across the tracks. "Help, Sergeant Preston, I'm tied to the tracks!"

He laughed and scooped her up. "I make this rescue at great risk to my own life. Now that I've saved you from an untimely death—"

She was leaning into him, very light-headed, wrapping her arms around his neck for support, not believing what she was doing. "No. The train only comes on Thursday afternoons."

"It might be late," he said.

She got a sudden, very aware sense of his masculinity, and pulled away. He let her go.

"Would you like to see the famous whirlpool?" she asked. He followed her as she stepped off the end of the bridge and down the bank to a spot almost below the bridge between a piling and a large, ancient weeping willow. The river took a bend underneath the bridge, sending it into a slow swirl after it left the rocks upstream. "We used to swim

here when we were kids. Everyone said if you got too close
to the center, you'd get sucked all the way to China, but
of course no one ever was, because the water is only four
feet deep. It was one of those things you say when you're
a kid. Did you say anything like that in Virginia?"

"Yes, indeed. In my neighborhood we said that if you
cut yourself between your thumb and your index finger,
you'd bleed to death immediately."

"Yes? Well, I'll show you something that really *is* true."
She ducked under the willow wands and tugged at one of
the plants that grew there. "This is bloodroot. The Indians
used it to dye their faces and tomahawks." Brushing aside
the trailing leaves, he looked at the scarlet juice dripping
from the broken ends of the stem in her hand. "When we
were kids, Renee and I and—" she hesitated, realizing she
had almost said David—"and our friends used to smear it
on our faces when we played settler maiden captured by the
Indian warriors."

As she spread the dye on his upraised palm and daubed
it around with a tapered fingertip, he said, "And what did
the warriors do to the captured maiden?"

"Oh, the unspeakable! She had to pound their clothes
clean on the rocks, haul water, scrape hides, wait on them
hand and foot."

Laughing, he laid his hands on her shoulders and pulled
her to him. "Kathy," he said. "This will sound sudden . . .
Will you come with me to Chicago and spend the weekend?"

His words brought a vague stab of sobriety. "Chicago?"
She put her palms against his chest and pushed a space
between them. "Is that a come-on?"

With one hand, he drew her gently back until their bodies
were lightly touching, and brought her chin up, his forefinger crooked underneath. In a whisper that nuzzled her, he
said, "Lady, I've been coming on to you since five o'clock
this afternoon. *That* was a proposition."

And then he kissed her, a brushing kiss first. She had
her hands still flat on his chest, but found herself, surprisingly, standing on tiptoes to meet him until she realized
what she was doing and made herself flat-footed again.

"No Chicago," she said breathlessly. "No propositions.
Why me?"

"If I told you, I'd frighten you again." She looked frightened, her eyes wide in the moonlight, and he brought his face down to the graceful curve of her neck and shoulder. "You smell like such an angel."

She pushed him again, more forcefully this time. It wasn't him she was struggling against, it was her warm, burning desire to press herself against him and feel all his hard length. She had never felt quite this way about a man, not even David.

"No," she moaned and took a step back. Her heel lit on a clump of turf and she stumbled against the bridge. He caught her up and brought his mouth back to hers, ruthlessly this time, plundering the silken treasure of her mouth. She felt his tongue lightly darting over her lips, touching the sensitive membranes on the inside of her cheek. She'd never been kissed like that before, and the hard drive of his questing kiss made her feel her control was being stretched to the breaking point.

"I don't know you." The remaining part of her sanity, which seemed to be shrinking rapidly, realized that the slow, sensual whisper was her own.

"Oh, but you will, you will," he answered. She felt his hands on her back, under the sweaters, against her skin. It felt warm and good. She felt his breathing quicken at the contact. He spoke; she didn't quite catch his words.

"What was that?" she breathed. "Mmmm."

"I said you feel soft and sweet, like a peach under the sun, like a lily petal . . ." His hands slipped upward, and she found herself lifting her arms enough to allow him to pull her sweaters over her head. In a deft movement he draped his leather jacket over her shoulders. And then his hand was back, his mouth never leaving hers as he moved aside the slender strap of her camisole top, and then, suddenly, arrestingly, arousingly, his fingertips were making a slow, circular motion around the tip of her breast. He drew her to the riverbank, cradling her in his arms on top of him, holding her to him with a hand resting on the curving swell of her hip.

Nothing in her experience had prepared her for a man like Neil Stratton. There was a persistent shocked disbelief in her mind that she was letting him do these things to her, but the thought was blocked from full consciousness by the incredible heat of their embrace. She felt his muscular chest rise and fall underneath her own softness, and pressed her cheek against his collarbone, her lips slightly parted. And then his mouth was in her gold hair, his tongue stroking over her ear. Her long legs were draped over his, and she felt him hard beneath her, and began to move restlessly against him. He put his hand tenderly to her cheek and stroked it, and then spread his fingers and stroked them back into her hair, pulling her face slowly toward his, covering her mouth again with his own, bringing his other hand up to steady her, her hair cascading down his sinewy forearms in a light wave, the shimmering ends falling on his cheeks. He traced the outline of her lips with his kiss, and then moved them to trace the bridge of her nose across the arch of her eyebrow to her temple.

"Say my name, Kathy," he whispered.

She was shivering, but not from the night air. "Why?"

"You haven't said it." He crushed his lips to hers urgently, drew them back, brought them down again. "Say it, Kathy—say my name. My first name."

"Neil," she said. "Neil."

He moved a little and she wrapped her arms around his neck. He pressed her to him, his palm broad and kneading on her hip, and held her mouth on his with his other hand on the back of her head.

"Are you still afraid, Kathy?"

Her mind felt like it was floating, floating in a sadness that grew at his words. "I think so . . . You were right about me being—intoxicated."

His tongue, moving on her cheek, found wetness. "You're crying." He took her hand in his own and pressed it to the tear streak. She wondered at the dampness there as he carefully shifted her from him, and rolled gently on top of her, letting the moonlight show him her face.

"How long has it been for you?" he asked her softly.

The intimacy of his question was rawly electric on her exposed emotions. Humiliated by her own childish lack of control, she said, "Do you mean how long has it been since I've been laid?" It was an expression she never used.

"No one would ever 'lay' you, Kathy. You're the kind of woman a man makes love to." He gazed down at her, checking her closely, his eyes wandering over her face, her trembling lip, the tears that were now beginning to well steadily from her brown eyes. And without another word he sat up next to her, helped her to pull on her sweaters, and brought her to her feet. He led the way to the car, his hand on her elbow to steady her as they walked up the bank and over the bridge, and held open the door again. He didn't have to ask her for directions to town. She closed her eyes and felt the smooth acceleration of the car as it picked up speed on the highway. Once she stole a glance at him as he drove. His face looked thoughtful in the blue light from the dashboard.

Broad Street was deserted when he pulled up in front of her shop. He got out, opened the car door for her, and she stood and shivered in spite of the bulky sweater as he unlocked the shop and flipped the light switch. He hung the key back on its nail, and then, just before leaving, walked into the back hall and threw open the window there to dispel the faint odor of glue that hung in the air. And then he walked past her as she stood by the counter, her head down. Like that, he was going to leave? But he paused by the door and turned. She felt his gaze on her and looked up. He was quiet for a moment, and reached out to touch her cheek, then turned to leave. But her words stopped him.

"Now you won't have a Wisconsin sticker for your suitcase," she said. "That's why you came back tonight, wasn't it? How did you put it—to experience the scenery?"

When he turned around again he had the half-smile, and his pale blue eyes pierced her like a spear. "Oh, lady, you underrate yourself. But I would have needed more time than a weekend in Chicago to do anything about that."

The cool insolence with which he spoke made the breath catch painfully in her throat. "So you chose to forgo the scenery?"

"I'd rather forgo it than leave it scarred behind me, particularly if the scenery was too tipsy to know what she was doing. How could I ruthlessly seduce a girl who knows every song in *Camelot* by heart? Don't worry about it, alright? It was all my fault. Your first instincts were correct. Sleep well, Kathy Carter."

He left. Kathy didn't want to watch the Mercedes disappear. She just stood by the door with her forehead against the frame.

3

Six weeks had passed since the day Neil Stratton had blazed through Kathy's life like a bright flare of a comet upon a placid horizon. But whatever else seemed to have gone out of her life since Neil's brief advent in it, it looked as though rock 'n' roll was here to stay. Exit Neil Stratton, enter Freddie and the Firecrackers.

The one recording studio in Apple Grove bore the name "Fritz's Audio Art and Appliance Shack Limited." "Shack" was too harsh a word to describe the neat frame building on the two-lane highway at the edge of town, and Fritz Waller, the proprietor, had a far from limited stock of eggbeaters and microwave ovens in the front of the store. Kathy could only conclude that "limited" referred to the "Audio Art." The smallish recording studio in the back, with its little closet of a control booth, was usually rented by Fritz to polka bands for the reasonable sum of ten dollars an hour. Folks in Apple Grove said there were only three things that Fritz Waller really liked—his mother back in Stuttgart, the polka, and quiet afternoons. So Kathy was resigned to his disappearance every time she arrived with Freddie and the Firecrackers, half-agreeing with Fritz's muttered curses as he brushed by on his way to Tony's, where he would sit drinking beer until they left.

Freddie and the Firecrackers were a three-man rock band from the Walworth County School for Boys, an institution set in the rolling countryside about eight miles from Apple Grove which, in a less enlightened age five years previously, had been known as the Walworth County Reform School for Delinquent Boys. A year and a half ago, when Kathy's father had taken on the volunteer chaplaincy there, her sister Renee had predicted that dear old Dad would be trying, sooner or later, to get the two of them involved. The school's latest problem was the leaky roof over the library. Melting snow had seeped through the rafters and destroyed most of the books over a warm weekend in early spring. There was no money in the budget to make repairs on the roof, or to buy more books, for that matter.

"But there is a way out," Kathy's dad said, with an optimistic look on his naïve and saintly face. "There are three musically inclined boys in the school, and they have themselves a little rock and roll band called Freddie and the Firecrackers. One of these young fellows came to me and suggested raising money for the school by making a recording of their band, and having a dance at which admission could be charged and the record could be sold, all the profits to be donated to the school. Needless to say, I felt such enterprise should be encouraged to the utmost! Mr. Waller has agreed to donate some time at his recording studio—" Fritz Waller was a member of her father's church and always behind on his tithe—"but we still need an advisor who knows about music. Kathy, didn't you study recording at the University?"

"Only a little, Dad," Kathy had said, feeling the start of a pre-volunteer headache. "And recording rock music requires highly specialized techniques."

For her part, Renee had been vociferously indignant. "Daddy, you can't be seriously considering exposing Kathy to those hoodlums of yours!"

Her father had looked so crestfallen that Kathy, an incurable soft touch, had called him later that day and offered her help. He had been voluble in his delight, and that left her with a warm glow which lasted halfway through the first recording session, when she began to realize that she had made a terrible mistake, and also that it was too late to back out.

That had been four sessions ago. And here they were still, with no significant progress toward a recording that sounded like anything more than a cannon shooting knives and forks through a plate glass window. But at least they hadn't stolen her purse, Kathy thought, and blew upward to dislodge some strands of blond hair that had fallen from the clasp at the back of her head as she leaned over the guitar on the studio floor.

Freddie and the Firecrackers. Kathy had begun—heaven help her!—to grow fond of them, which meant either that even the least appealing young have a way of endearing themselves to their elders as a way of insuring the survival of the species, or that she was a sap.

An amplifier fuse had blown. While Mike and Eric, respectively bass and lead guitar players, were checking the wiring, Kathy was replacing a worn string on the bass.

Glancing sideways at the drums, she saw that Sticks appeared to have gone to sleep. Of course, he always appeared to be asleep when he wasn't drumming. The boy was leaning on the back legs of his stool, head against the wall, the drumsticks stuck in his shirt pocket, his unruly brownish hair hanging down over his eyes. The lower part of his face was obscured by acne, the variety and profusion of which could have provided enough material for a five-pound dermatology textbook. Sticks, her father had told her, was from a close-knit backwoods family from northern Wisconsin. With his three older brothers, he had broken into a lumberyard office one night, and tried to open the safe with a crowbar. When that didn't work, they had carried the safe out of the building and dumped it bodily into the trunk of their car. Unfortunately, they couldn't get the trunk lid closed over it and the county sheriff stopped them before they'd gone five miles.

Rarely had Sticks spoken to Kathy beyond those poignant occasions when he tilted back his head to gaze at her from under his fuzzy bangs and said, "Got any gum?"

Mike did most of the talking. Mike was a seventeen-year-old electronics wizard whose affluent parents had bought him a modest home computer, which he'd illicitly transformed into a lucrative enterprise involving mysterious activities with blue boxes, specially coded pushbutton phones, and the inter-bank transfer of funds. Even the prosecuting attorney hadn't been able to figure out how Mike had done it. But when a kid with an allowance of ten dollars a week turns up with a thirty thousand dollar bank account under a false name . . . Mike was the band's organizer and prime force, and to Kathy he was unfailingly polite and unflinchingly patient, even when she asked such foolish questions as why the group was named Freddie and the Firecrackers when there wasn't a Freddie in the group. With Mike's glib tongue and sharklike ethics, Kathy had no doubt that the boy would end his days as the president of a major corporation.

And then there was Eric Carpenter. The guitar string snapped back at her, lashing painfully into the back of Kathy's hand, drawing blood. "Ow!" she said softly. Eric had the all-American-surfer sort of good looks, the blue-eyed blond look that seems dumb but isn't. Eric was the authority-hating product of a strict disciplinarian father. Kathy knew she was in for trouble the first time Eric took off his shirt and she saw that he had a marijuana plant tattooed on one arm. He had been the leader of a street gang in Milwaukee. The superintendent at the boys' school had shown her the record of his crimes when he interviewed her about overseeing the project. She didn't even want to think about some of the things Eric had done. "He needs a friend," her father had said. What Eric needed, Kathy thought, was a contingent of National Guardsmen in full battle regalia to surround him everywhere he went.

Right now there was a cigarette dangling from his lips as he worked on the amplifier and the ashes were dropping on the floor. Kathy dreaded having to say: "Don't drop ashes on the carpet, Eric. Fritz doesn't like it." She stared in frustrated fascination at his lengthening ash, and when it finally fell, she put the guitar aside, picked up a glass ashtray and whapped it down on the speaker at Eric's elbow.

He glanced at it, and then at her, with a piranha's smile. "You shouldn't have!" He flicked his ash on the carpet next to the speaker. "Damn, I missed."

It was another challenge to her, one more in a long line of challenges. Determined not to let him get the best of her, she snatched the cigarette from his fingers and dropped it, still burning, into his half-full bottle of Coke, where it sizzled into soggy carbon.

He turned with startling quickness, his lips twisted in an angry sneer. "Ain't it just something," he said sarcastically, "how uppity a chick gets when she's once got into Neil Stratton's pants?"

Kathy's blush was instant and all-inclusive—neck, cheeks, ears. Had the rumors reached even to these kids? Eric had never given her any sign that he knew. Stored ammo; probably he'd been saving it for just the right occasion. Clearly he was relishing her blushes.

"Go gargle with your acne scrub," she snapped, marching past him into the control room and jerking the door closed behind her. Mike exclaimed, "Eric, you moron! How much more of that do you think she's going to put up with?"

Drat that Carpenter kid. Again he had gotten her into a childish squabble and, as usual, he gave better than he got. Kathy's shoulders sagged. Letting out a slow exhalation, she dropped into the cane-bottom chair and gazed through the small glass panel into the room she'd left.

Mike was lecturing Eric, who stared upward and looked as though he were counting the holes in the acoustical tiles. Finally Eric shrugged and said something that made Mike laugh and slap him on the arm. They turned their attention back to the amplifier.

There. Another brush with what Renee liked to call the Neil Stratton episode. Rumors about her meeting with the famous singer had hung around the community for weeks, gradually waning, but ever mouth-watering, like old Halloween candy. If only Mary Beth Powers, the most popular beautician in town, hadn't seen Kathy getting into a fancy red car at midnight with a handsome stranger. And if only Kathy had been able to hold out against Mary Beth's persistent questions about the identity of that stranger. Well, repent at leisure, they say. They were so right. People she hadn't talked to in years had scurried to their attics to discover old instruments to bring to her as an excuse to visit and interrogate her about Stratton. Kathy had been presented with everything from fifty-year-old piccolos to recorders that some long-gone dog had chewed almost in half. Neil Stratton's stardust rubbed off too easily on anyone around him.

To top things off, Kathy discovered that she'd developed a secret obsession with the man. It had begun innocently enough, when she'd borrowed Renee's car for the fifty-mile drive to the capital city to pick up an off-sized dent mandrel from a supplier, and had ended in a trip to the main library there, where, in the anonymity of the big-city ambience, she had spent four hours reading every magazine article written about Neil Stratton in the last ten years.

She learned that Stratton owned a villa in Los Angeles valued at a million dollars five years ago, as well as a penthouse in New York City, a rustic hideaway in Tennessee whose location was a well-guarded secret, and a custom-built bus for touring that had fifteen-century Dutch engravings on the walls. He gave to a smorgasbord of causes, and the word "liberal" described both the generosity of the contributions and the philosophical bent of the recipients. Well, alright, she thought. In America everyone is entitled to his opinion. Worse by far were his women. Every month there seemed to be a new one more beautiful than the one before. January—the congressman's ex-wife; February—the publishing magnate's daughter; March—female lead of a prime-time sitcom; and there was Neil beside them, getting out of limousines and going into posh nightclubs, roller discos, Broadway openings. Two weeks after his appearance at Kathy Carter's Instrument Repair Shop, he had flown to Paris on the invitation of a fashion designer girlfriend ten years older than he was, so the article gleefully pointed out. The accompanying photograph showed him draped with blonde models, one kissing his ear, the other biting his finger. When a reporter had asked him what he liked to see his women wearing, Neil Stratton had said, "My bathrobe."

Placed against her memory of sitting beside him in a car singing *Camelot* off-key, there was something about the combination that made her want to sink into the library seat with the magazine over her head. And later—if only she'd stuck to singing! It probably made a great anecdote for him over sushi at Malibu beach parties.

Many times while she was working on her instruments or listening to a poorly prepared piano lession, her imagination carried her back to that night and she could feel the feather touch of his lips on her throat, the ache of her breasts inside his gentle grip, and the breathtaking crush of their lacing bodies. She was horrified by the ease with which she had nearly given herself to him. Why had it never been like that with David, when they had loved each other so dearly? Why?

"We're all set." There were two doors to the control booth, one at her back, which led into the shop, and one at the side, where Mike was now standing, tapping his booted foot impatiently. "You didn't see us waving at you through the window. I hope Eric didn't upset you too much. I wish there was some way to make him shut up."

"There is," she said. "But it's called manslaughter." Donning the headphones, she added brightly, "I'm ready."

Mike went back into the studio and strapped on his guitar, giving the high sign to the other two. Kathy rolled tape, and they began to play. And it was more of the same frustration—thin vocals, lead guitar either too loud or too soft—disaster. They would stop, Kathy would play the tape back, they would make volume adjustments or move the drum set around farther to the back, closer to the front. But nothing helped.

Finally the tinkering stopped, and the positioning of the drums and guitar players in relation to each other. Things were about as good as they were going to get, and besides, Fritz would return in two hours, and an hour had already gone by with only half a song recorded. Kathy dimmed the light in the control booth, told the boys through the intercom to go ahead after the count of ten, and pushed the RECORD button. The brown inch-wide band of tape began slipping across the machine heads between the two slowly revolving wheels, and the band thundered into its number.

Maybe it was a trick of her mood, but the music didn't sound half bad today. She had always rather liked this song and they had improved it considerably in the past week. Her foot began to discover and tap to the understated reggae beat. Another minute passed and she was humming along. Then—what the heck—she began to snap her fingers.

For a few finger-snapping moments she thought she was alone. Then her peripheral vision saw movement beside her, and she turned her head. Her nose was two inches from a hip, a beautifully shaped and slender male hip, firm and high-boned, casually encased in denim. Her eyes traveled upward over the lean midriff seen through a thin white cotton shirt, over the suntanned neck and upper chest revealed by the open collar, over the cleft chin with the tiny scar on it, and the lazily smiling lips, and warm light blue eyes that greeted her glance. And the hair, well-cut, brown, shining.

Neil Stratton.

"Help!" she said, her faint cry drowned under the growl of electric guitars. Every sense organ froze briefly and then melted to warm cream under the caress of his smile. One forgot, looking at him in slick magazine stills, what that smile was capable of doing to even the steadiest pulse and respiration.

His strong musician's fingers plucked one earphone away from her ear and, leaning over with his lips close to her cheek, he said, "Don't faint."

His smile deepened. "Remember me? The one who wanted you to adjust his tuning peg?"

Kathy received a clean drift of fragrance from his hair as he replaced the earphone. In a movement that was easy and graceful, he settled his long body tidily on the Formica countertop next to the control panel. In the meantime she had dragged off her headphones, letting them lie like a collar around her neck.

"What are you doing here?" she managed through vocal cords that had somehow developed a tremolo effect.

Stratton bent forward slightly. Reaching out, his fingertips stroked the back of her hand where it lay clenched into a white-knuckled fist on her knee. Moving gently, he slipped a single finger over her thumb and inside the warm, quivering tunnel of her fingers. Holding her hand as though it were a flower, he drew it to his lips, and without lifting his bright, charismatic gaze from her eyes, he pressed a soft kiss on the base of her fingers. The touch of his lips ran like hot oil down her arm, through her dilating veins, and into the sensitive depths of her body.

"I went to your shop," he said. "Your sister told me where to find you."

Renee was minding the shop for Kathy this afternoon. Trust her to give him directions. So her sister had met him! Kathy wondered what they had thought of each other.

Before she could ask, he picked up the headphones from her neck and spread them, saying, before he slipped them over her ears again, "I don't want to distract you. We'll talk later." He seated them snugly over her ears, making sure not to catch her hair, and she remembered resentfully how masterful he could be.

She turned her gaze out the viewing window toward the band again. The Firecrackers were involved in a long instrumental section. She could feel Neil Stratton studying her, reading her face like an artist, deciphering the lines and planes in a search for clues to her personality. It was distinctly unnerving, just what she was beginning to expect from anything concerned with him.

Squealing feedback suddenly assaulted her ears, and her hands flew to the headphones as she grimaced in pain. He observed what she was doing, and reached out to flip a switch on the panel—a switch she had never been particularly aware of—and the feedback magically ceased. There was a pad of paper and a pencil on the control panel; he wrote on it in big letters: "O.K. now?"

She nodded and gave him a sudden nervous smile. Neil Stratton responded with a slow, deep curl of the lips, the smile that was voted the most photogenic of the year by the International News Photographers Association. Reaching out a finger, he gently touched her chin. Again she felt the full voltage of a charisma which beguiled its way into the senses and kidnapped the emotions. The blue eyes covered her in a sweet and delicate gaze as his fingers passed over the curve of her face and stroked softly under her jaw. Lightheaded from his finger-play, she told herself grimly: Keep a grip on it, Kathy girl.

The music came to an abrupt halt. Mike's exasperated voice filtered into Kathy's ears through the headphones: "Once, Carpenter, just *once,* I wish you'd play a song the same way twice. Where'd you get that riff, Duane Eddy?"

"What's wrong with that?" Eric shot back belligerently. "I *like* Duane Eddy!"

In the control room, Kathy shook her head.

"Here we go again," she said. At first she had tried to help them settle their disputes. It hadn't taken long to realize that they settled things more quickly when she left them alone. She stopped the tape and switched off the feed from the studio. Neil gently removed the headphones from her ears and set them in front of her. She stared at them intently, took a deep breath, and when she thought her larynx would work right, she said a second time, "What *are* you doing here?"

"Hmmm." His expression was frank and beguiling as he seemed to think over his answer. "Have you read *Peter Pan?* There was an alligator in the story who bit off the hand of an old pirate called Captain Hook, and the 'gator liked the taste of him so much that he chased Hook around until the end of the story, wanting to have the rest of him." As a band of pink color began to spread over the bridge of her nose, he added, "Don't look so frightened. I promise to proceed by gentle nibbles."

That did it. Her blood ran so hot that she wouldn't be surprised if it was raising blisters on the surfaces of her veins. What in heaven's name was he trying to do to her? She sat very still listening to the roar of her heartbeat and staring at five feet eleven inches, one hundred and sixty pounds (if the magazines were right about his vital statistics) of heartbreak-about-to-happen.

"Men like you," she said slowly, "ought to be compelled by law to wear a sign that reads: 'Caution—this male may be hazardous to your emotional health.' I thought you weren't coming back. What happened to your chivalrous impulses?"

"There's no cause for alarm, Kathy Carter. All chivalrous impulses are fully operational." He gave her the smile again. "I've thought of better ways to be nice to you."

Her heart was galloping ahead of her brain. She continued to stare at him helplessly. Kindly, nodding toward the window, he changed the subject. "Is the rest of their stuff this good?"

Was he being sarcastic? "Good?" she repeated. "You think they're good? I know they're talented; I'd love to have one-eighth of their musical talent. But good?"

"I'll have to hear more," he said, "but for a three-member band of high school kids, they seem about as good as they come." Then, "They need a drum booth," he added.

"Do they?" she said. "What's a drum booth?"

"You put up soundproofing screens around the drums— it keeps the sound of the drums from bleeding into the other mikes, and vice versa. In some studios the drum booth is a little room all its own, like a little padded cell—appropriate for most drummers."

Diabolical. The man was truly diabolical. Freddie and the Firecrackers were the most difficult problem area in her life, and here was Neil Stratton dangling solutions from his gold-mine storehouse of technical expertise over her head like a baited fishhook. He was twenty-four-carat temptation. But it was important to remember, when one is dealing with comets, that no matter how dazzling they are, they never stay long. And some were like Kahoutek—months of promise, and then nothing. She must try very hard to resist taking this man too seriously . . . She must.

She forced herself to think about a drum booth. What would Fritz do if she moved in a load of lumber and began to saw and hammer up a little room in the corner of his studio? Probably attack her with one of his eggbeaters . . .

"I like the padded cell idea," she said. "But could we build it around the lead guitar instead?"

He looked at her quizzically before he leaned to the side to gaze out the window into the studio. The loose gauzy weave of his shirt strained over the straight line of his back and outlined the strength in his shoulders. Softly contrasting with the hardness below it, his hair brushed like heavy satin fibers over his crisp collar. He turned back. "Does the kid give you trouble?"

"The *kid* gives me ulcers."

"Mouthy?"

"Calling Eric Carpenter mouthy is like saying a cannibal is a man with varied appetites." There it was again—the incredible incongruity. She was talking about the minor details of her life with a man who had stepped out of the pages of a magazine, out of nearly ten years of remembered music, and, since she had met him two months before, out of her dreams.

Neil Stratton pushed himself from the counter and stood. "There now. I've got a handle on the *second* nice thing I can do for Kathy Carter. We'll lay down a little sound-deadening material in the right places." He put his hand on the doorknob.

"Neil, wait! What are you going to do?"

"Nothing to be concerned about," he said. "I only intend to barrel full tilt into your life and solve your problems until you've developed an unbreakable dependence on me." He started to twist the doorknob.

"Neil, those aren't three run-of-the-mill teenagers out there. They're—"

"I know," he said. "Your sister told me." His smile was intimate. "Relax. I know how to talk to kids."

The incredible thing was, he did. She watched him through the window. Whatever she would have expected from him, it was still a surprise to see that within twenty minutes of introducing himself he had them wrapped around his little finger. That he was Neil Stratton helped him for the first five minutes; after that, she knew, he was on his own. With friendly confidence and a sense of humor, he got them beyond the star-struck stage, and soon they were talking relievedly with him about their technical problems.

The second surprise was that they were willing to take his advice. Usually they were so touchy they wouldn't even listen to each other. Careful analysis of Stratton's methods revealed to Kathy that at least part of his success was due to being able to cleverly conceal advice within dazzlingly well-told anecdotes about recording with other music business greats. Not the kind of thing she could co-opt for her own use.

Fritz Waller came in through the appliance shop door, harrumphed at Kathy by way of a greeting, and peered through the window into the studio. "Hey! Who's the young fella in with those punks of yers?"

"That's Neil Stratton, Mr. Waller. He's a—"

"Stratton! I know who he is! Took you riding in some swell red car this spring, didn't he, when he came to Nordic Valley? Big shot movie star and be-bop-a-doodle singer, ain't he?"

"He has starred in a couple of movies, Mr. Waller," Kathy offered cautiously, scenting trouble. "But I don't think that 'be-bop-a-doodle' accurately describes the type of music that—"

"Sleazeballs! Them kind of guys is no good. I don't know what's the matter with that father of yers, letting you hang around with these punks and sleazeballs. You stay in here, Mrs. Carter. I'm gonna have a word or two with Mr. Big Shot."

Not only did Kathy stay in the control room, she felt a strong compulsion to hide under the tape recorder. Fritz Waller vs. Neil Stratton. For twenty minutes she couldn't bring herself to turn on the sound or look into the adjoining room. Then, turning up the volume of the studio feed and peeking into the studio, Kathy was confronted with the spectacle of Neil Stratton leading Freddie and the Firecrackers and Fritz Waller, beaming toothily over the pleats of his accordion, laughing their way through "The E-I-E-I-O Polka."

4

KATHY HAD SPENT the morning eradicating the cheerful reminders of a wedding from her father's church. Daddy had planned to get to the job this afternoon, but she and Renee had conspired to "give the old gentleman a little time off," as Renee put it. While her sister took charge of the shop, Kathy wiped handprints from the stained glass, swept up rice and stray bits of ribbon, collected forgotten lipsticks, and folded chairs from the reception, putting them into their back-room rack. They were activities well suited to Kathy's state of mind, because they provided the perfect backdrop for her to brood upon the ironies of the mating and marriage ritual, and the tricks it played on its innocent participants.

June had settled like a steam blanket on Apple Grove. Sleek sunshine winked through the gingerbread trim on the Victorian houses she passed on Broad Street as she strolled back toward her shop. Young leaves sparkled on the untrimmed oaks as they threw shadows on the cracked sidewalk below. Two small boys were playing in a rotating sprinkler head, their bare feet dancing gaily over golden dandelions. A trembling rainbow hung in the spray above the pavement. Kathy walked through it, shivering in delight

45

as the cold droplets pricked her skin. Giving a cordial wave
to Mrs. Harrison, who was mowing her lawn across the
street, she sidestepped the newspaper girl who was pulling
her stack of papers along the sidewalk in a red wagon.

The line of trees ended as Kathy neared the three-block
downtown area. She pulled her sunglasses from the top of
her head and stuck them on her nose. Perhaps the heat was
responsible for her disquiet this morning. A vague but persistent restlessness had settled on her for some days now.
She wished something would happen. That was coupled
with the not-so-vague worry that Neil Stratton was what she
wanted to happen.

He had come twice, for long sessions, since that time
a month ago, to help Freddie and the Firecrackers. *That* at
least was working out very well. The tracks the band had
laid down were immeasurably improved with Neil's suggestions. "Almost like a real record," the boys had said. It
was a small miracle how their sound had emerged from the
primordial mud through Neil's technical expertise. He had
shown them how to plug the recording lines into the speaker
jacks of the amplifiers and how to mike each cymbal sep-
arately so the individual recording volume could be varied.
And he had made suggestions about their material as well,
encouraging Eric to work in the country and western riffs
he liked, showing Sticks how to coordinate the bass drum
with Mike's bass guitar. And Neil had helped Mike arrange
the ballads he wrote, until they were beginning to sound
almost pretty.

Kathy's early fear had been that Neil would immediately
try to seduce her. She was still far from figuring him out.
Wasn't that why he had come back? And yet after that first
moment together in the recording booth, he hadn't been
alone with her. Nor had he made any sign in front of the
others that he intended more with her than friendship. There
were times when she almost began to believe that herself,
and that conclusion left her quietly depressed, though only
God knew why it should. There were women aplenty who
might have the stuffing for a hot, uncommitted relationship
with a superstar, but she was not among them. When she
was with him, she was high and happy. But as soon as he
left, the fear returned, like stepping from sunlight into shade.
If she was ever so foolish as to give herself to him, she

knew she would learn to know that shade well. His life was a full calendar of commitments to other people in places that were far away and unfamiliar to her.

For the month he was living in Los Angeles where, with another music business great, he was scoring a film. He flew into Wisconsin on a chartered jet and drove to Apple Grove. When she had pointed out in an appalled way that such a thing must be costing him a fortune, he had looked at her with those astonishingly warm eyes and the smile of a man whose semi-annual royalties could have bought Kathy's home county, and said kindly, "Darlin', I can afford it."

Anyway, the project was the important thing.

It was a dream come true for the boys to get help from Neil Stratton, and the fact that he wasn't pressuring her for any kind of a relationship should have left her relieved instead of half-sick with unresolved longing. The prospect of an afternoon in her stuffy, hot shop spent on detail work with an old violin, trying to ignore her feelings, was not an inviting one, and she walked slowly down Broad Street as it hummed pleasantly before her.

The Fourth of July flags were up early and waving. Lifelong friends and neighbors came and went from the bank and post office. The firemen were washing the hook and ladder truck in front of the fire station. And the bright orange van from Bill's Hardware was parked in front of her shop. Bill himself, on a ladder, was knocking a hole in her wall . . . *Knocking a hole in her wall?*

She had never made it down Broad Street so fast. Her ankle straps disappeared under her heels as she ran, and her sandals flew off as she arrived at the ladder, where Bill whistled to the clatter of the hammers and wrenches hanging from the loops in his overalls.

"Bill Harding, what are you doing?" Kathy managed as soon as she caught her breath, wincing from the pain of a sideache.

Renee was in the doorway, leaning against the frame, looking smashing in a flowered sundress. "For goodness' sake, quit squawking like an excited chicken, Kath. He's just installing your new ventilation system."

"Ventilation system? What ventilation system? I didn't order a ventilation system," Kathy choked out.

"It's on my list," said Bill from the top of the ladder, and paused to take a phlegmatic bite out of his cigar. Randy Newley, his assistant, stuck his scrawny neck through the hole from inside and said, grinning, "You'll have to take it anyway, 'less ya want the rain comin' in the hole."

"Darn it all, I don't want it," said Kathy with spirit. "You're going to have to repair that hole! I didn't order a ventilation system. I can't afford one. I can hardly meet my bills as it is! Show me my signature on the order."

Bill came slowly and carefully down the ladder, placing both feet on one rung at the same time before going down to the next one, as was prudent for a man of his bulk. Kathy chewed on her thumbnail and waited for him impatiently. The landlady was going to kill her—she'd make her pay for the damage. Disaster. Renee left the doorway to put her arm around Kathy's shoulders.

"Calm down, kid," she said in her best soothing big-sister way. But that didn't help very much. Kathy was seeing red, and felt ill from a welter of emotions. "It's all my fault, really," Renee was continuing. "If someone has to pay for something, I'll do it. I was surprised you hadn't mentioned it, but these two seemed so convinced . . ."

Now Renee was getting upset, and Kathy decided to be stoically calm to save her sister's feelings. Renee immediately looked relieved at her sister's new demeanor, and they both waited for what seemed forever as Bill, now earthbound, rummaged through his many voluminous pockets, pulling out little pieces of paper of all hues in the spectrum, slowly reading them with great concentration. Finally he found the right one.

"Here's your permit slip, signed by the landlady." He showed it to them, stuck it back in his pocket, and rummaged some more. A stray piece of carbon fell from his hands and blew away. "And here's the order, marked paid by charge, with the receipt."

Kathy snatched it from his ham-like hand and held it up to the sun, trying to make out the purchaser's name. It was a Los Angeles address, the street name illegible. "Sunrise Corporation?"

"Never heard of it," said Renee.

"Who could that be? Do you know who it is?" Kathy asked the two workmen.

"Dunno, dunno, dunno who it is," was the rumbling duet of an answer. Randy Newley had not stopped grinning at her, but then, he had never stopped grinning at anyone in the fifteen years she had known him.

"I'm going to get to the bottom of this," Kathy snapped, and brushed past them into the shop. She snatched up the phone, not realizing that she was standing on the cord. The pressure on the receiver tightened as she dragged it toward her ear, and she watched in startled confusion as the phone seemed to leap from her hand to the floor with an angry jangle and split open its case to disgorge a rolling collection of mechanical parts.

Kathy bent slowly and picked up the mouthpiece. Dead. To the three peering at her through the doorway, she said dangerously, "Don't you *dare* laugh at me."

Undeterred, she intended to stalk from the shop to make the telephone call next door, but she stubbed her toe on a trumpet case, so her entrance into Ye Sweete Shoppe next door was made hopping on one foot and muttering mild expletives.

The glass in Ye Sweete Shoppe's antique phone booth had been missing since "Hound Dog" was a gleam in Elvis Presley's eye. Every teenager in the shop stopped eating in mid-bite, belly-busting burgers poised halfway to orthodontured teeth as Kathy spun out the numbers for directory information in Los Angeles, California on the old clear plastic dial. Her sister arrived with the two men from Bill's Hardware.

"She already kilt her own phone," Randy Newley announced, grinning at Kathy's interested audience.

The L.A. operator answered and Kathy asked somewhat uncertainly for the number of Sunrise Corporation. She had barely finished speaking when the operator came back with the number. Renee yanked a ballpoint pen from Bill's pocket and wrote the number in red ink on the back of Randy's dusty coveralls as Kathy repeated it aloud, clicked the receiver, and dialed the number. But before the call went through, a long distance operator came on the line and rather irritably instructed Kathy to deposit two dollars and sixty cents.

"Two sixty, two sixty," Kathy repeated feverishly, holding her hand through the empty phone booth window. A small mound of dimes and quarters grew in her palm, donations from her chortling spectators. She jammed the money into the slot like a compulsive gambler playing a one-armed bandit.

"Sunrise Corporation," answered a feminine voice of singsong efficiency, with an underlying hint of steel.

"This is Kathy Carter calling from Wisconsin. There's a hole in my building because Sunrise Corporation has just—"

"One moment, please," said the voice, dripping honey. A series of sharp electronic snicks announced to Kathy that she had been placed on hold. She waited, tapping her foot angrily, getting advice and encouragement from the burgeoning crowd.

Finally she heard, "Linda Evans's office, my I help you?" This voice was less singsong, more efficient, and the underlying steel was more than a hint. So, she had been warned. Kathy opened her mouth to speak when the operator came back on the line and crossly ordered Kathy to deposit more money.

Kathy rammed four quarters and a nickel down the slot. "This is Kathy Carter calling from Apple Grove, Wisconsin. There's been some kind of mistake. A hole has been made in my building for a ventilation system which I didn't order, and your company's name is on the receipt."

A ten-second silence on the other end, then, "Would you repeat that, please?"

Kathy did, a little more slowly and patiently, but she might as well not have, because when she was done, the woman said, "You must have the wrong number, ma'am. We don't handle ventilation systems here. This is a music publishing company."

"That may well be, Miss Evans, but—"

"This is not Linda Evans. This is her secretary speaking."

"Whoever you are, your company has just knocked a hole in my building, or paid to have it done anyway. Let me speak to Miss Evans."

"I'm sorry, Miss Evans is not in right now. Would you like to speak with Mr. Brooks? If you hold on, I'll see if Mr. Brooks can talk to you." Kathy was put on hold again. The operator interrupted and demanded more money. Seething, Kathy threw in more coins. By the time whoever it was came back on the line again, the crowd around the little phone booth was five deep. "Mr. Brooks will speak to you now."

"Brooks." It might be a lot to derive from a voice, but Kathy was certain the speaker was young, deeply tanned, and had a zodiac charm dangling from a gold chain around his neck.

With real passion, Kathy repeated her story. She'd had enough practice by now to do a good job. And when she was finished, Brooks said meditatively, "Apple Grove, Apple Grove . . . Yeah, I remember now. Apple Grove. An order to a hardware store. Listen, Linda Evans got the note to set that up and she just left for Baja this morning, so I'm afraid there's not much that I can . . ." Then, in an objective tone, "So, you're a friend of Neil's?"

Neil Stratton. She might have known. She really should have known. And she didn't like the way Brooks said "friend." Very sweetly, Kathy asked, "Are you an employee of Neil Stratton's?"

"You might say so. This is his publishing company. I'll tell you what . . ."

"No, thank you. I'd like to speak to Mr. Stratton."

"I'm sorry, but he's not here," Brooks said. "And I can't give you another number for him because your name's not on the approved list. I've already checked. I don't know why it's not. Must be someone's oversight, because it should be there if you're one of Neil's ladies."

"I am *not* one of Neil's ladies," Kathy said furiously.

"Listen. Just hang loose, wait a few days, and I'm sure Neil will be in touch."

"At his own peril!" Kathy said, noting that the man's voice had become much kinder. Instinct told her she was not the first of "Neil's ladies" Brooks or Sunrise had dealt with. "Please inform Mr. Stratton that his name is not on *my* approved list."

"Want some free advice?" asked Brooks calmly. "Relax. Stay cool. Play things Neil's way or the man will tie you into more knots than a macrame plant hanger. Stratton gets what he wants. He wouldn't be where he is today if he didn't. Relax. Enjoy the guy."

Pink from ear to ear with wrathful indignation, Kathy was about to tell Mr. Brooks what she thought of his advice when the operator interrupted.

"Please deposit one dollar and eighty cents to cover the next three minutes."

With a groan Renee later referred to as demented, Kathy slammed down the phone.

She let them install the system. If people were going to drive by her shop wondering what was going on between her and Neil Stratton, a vent fan had ten times the discretion of a gaping hole nailed up with plywood. All she could do was wait for the weekend, when Neil was coming to help the boys, and then give him a piece of what was probably her rapidly deteriorating mind.

Saturday began badly. A long piano lesson made Kathy late to the studio. Fritz Waller was in the front of his store trying to sell a set of video games to an elderly couple who had come in to have their toaster repaired. He took the time to whisper to Kathy that Neil wasn't here yet either.

In the recording studio, Kathy discovered that Eric had finally succeeded in burning an ash-hole in the carpet. He did not take kindly to the stern lecture she delivered in reproof, and while she was trying distressedly to rub at the carpet spot with a Kleenex, she sat back on her heels to notice that Eric was grinning evilly at her chest. Glancing down at the soft denim jeans and the rather deeply cut yellow t-shirt with skinny straps she wore, she saw where the filigree butterfly on her necklace was fluttering. The necklace had been a Christmas present from Renee, and Kathy had only worn it with a high-necked sweater before, so it hadn't occurred to her that, when worn with a more revealing garment, it would nuzzle into her cleavage. There were hazards to leaving one's bedroom without looking into a full-length mirror.

"Nice necklace," Eric murmured.

Even Mike showed a disconcerting tendency to let his eyes wander while they talked. Of course, she could have taken the necklace off, but that would in a subtle way have given Eric the satisfaction of knowing that he had embarrassed her. The situation worsened considerably when she was helping Sticks move his drum set around to conceal the burned spot in the carpet; she picked up Eric's soda can from the floor and detected a heavy odor of alcohol.

"Liquor! You've got liquor in here!" She took a sip from the can, made a terrible face, and went to the little bathroom in the back to pour it down the sink, returning to shove the empty can into Eric's hand. "I can't believe you'd have the unmitigated gall to do something like this. You're a minor. If someone found out about this, it would be the end of the project, and you would be in a heck of a lot of trouble on your own account. Not to mention the trouble *I'd* be in!"

"Don't worry," Eric leered. "If they put you in Walworth you can share my bunk."

Neil Stratton sauntered through the studio door, coming in behind Eric just in time to hear the last remark. He directed a concerned glance at Kathy, caught her expression, and then planted the sole of one expensively handcrafted Western boot firmly on Eric's posterior and gave him a shove, sending him flying across the studio through the drum set, which clattered and banged around him as he sprawled on the floor after hitting the wall. One of the cymbals rolled noisily around on edge before vibrating to a stop. The other two band members gaped open-mouthed as Eric staggered to his feet, glaring at Neil and cursing.

"Can it, Eric," Neil snapped. "I hear worse from my road crew every morning on tour. You *will* treat this lady with respect. Mike, you go out and keep Fritz busy for a few minutes, so he doesn't come in and see this mess, and Sticks and Eric—you two clean it up." He waited a split second to make sure they were all doing as he had directed, and then pulled Kathy into the control booth and closed the door behind them.

"That kid," she gritted out, "makes me so mad—"

"I know," he said. "Don't worry. I'm working on him for you. I think when he gets out of Walworth, I'll find someone to make him a big rock star and he can play out his stud fantasies until he's blue in the face. A normal kid may yet emerge. Not, of course, that his yen for you represents any kind of abnormality. I have to admit I share his taste."

It was not so much what he said, but how he said it. Well, maybe it was a bit what he said. Kathy's skin began to prickle with gathering heat. Around her, the control room was dusky and quiet. A dark shade covered the studio window and dim ivory light curled around the corners. Tiny colored lights and bobbing dials shone star-like in the darkness. Neil, standing close to her in this high-tech womb, had a faint natural fragrance that was disturbingly human and male, and the rich material of his shirt cradled his shoulders luxuriously.

Ignoring, or at least not responding verbally to his final sentence, Kathy said, "Is that why you became who you are? To live out your fantasies?"

His laughter was husky and soft. "Maybe. The much-touted amenities never deterred anyone from learning to play the guitar." He lifted a fall of her hair and let it sift slowly from his fingers. "I'd better warn you that I have a fantasy or two yet to live out, and, darlin', you feature in them prominently. Why do you look at me like that? Am I such a monster?"

Pulling back her shoulders so that her hair slipped from his careful hold, fighting to subdue the frantic pace of her heartbeat, she said shakily, "Now see here, Mr. Stratton, I don't know what you're used to—" although she did have a pretty good idea—"but just because you happen to have more lines than a striped silk tie, that doesn't mean I'm going to fall limp at your feet." All at once, the image of the expensive new vent system winged into her mind. "And I'm *not* for sale."

His eyes brightened with merry devilment. "Does this mean the death of my hopes to cajole you into an improper relationship with me on the promise that I'll catapult Eric and company from reform school to stardom?"

"I happen to be serious, *Mr.* Stratton."

"I know that, *Ms.* Carter. I just thought that if I used a more Victorian mode of communication, we might be able to understand each other better."

"Are you saying that you think I'm old-fashioned?" she asked angrily, growing oddly disoriented by her conflicting desires to land a punch on his jaw and to touch her fingers lightly over his curving lips.

"Lady, you're fashioned just fine," he said. His fingers found and began to trace down the flesh beside her strap. He followed the action with his fond gaze, stopping less than a centimeter from the upper swell of her breast, and then transferred his hand and his eyes to her indignant face.

"Honesty compels me to admit that I know what's bothering you, Kathy. Jon Brooks called me this morning."

Kathy remembered the coolly pleasant Brooks without warmth. "Yes. The one who informed me roundly that Mr. Stratton wouldn't take my phone call."

"A miscalculation on his part, because Mr. Stratton will take phone calls day or night from a certain party in Apple Grove, Wisconsin. I'm sorry. If I'd known you were going to call me, I would have left word at Sunrise. I'd never have been so audacious as to think you might call. Next time they'll put you through."

"That's not the point," she said, fighting to stay angry. For five days solid the desire to read Neil Stratton the riot act had dominated her every waking minute. But in some way—too easily—he seemed to be taking the wind out of her sails. She had to build up her resistance to that sinfully easy charm and that disingenuous smile. She was not about to stay cool and play things his way. For once Stratton was not going to get everything he wanted. "I was calling to tell you that I didn't want— Neil, what in the world possessed you to buy me a vent fan?"

Stratton gave her a lazy grin. "I couldn't sleep nights, thinking about what could happen to you if a young man of shady intentions were to walk into your shop after you'd been exposed to concentrated glue vapors."

Kathy spent a moment doing the emotional equivalent to gnashing her teeth. Then she said, "Darn it all, Neil Stratton, what do you want from me? What are you going to expect in return?"

"What do I expect?" His hands came to her face and his palms felt cool and clean as they molded themselves to her cheeks and held her as though she were as fragile and perfect as a moss rose. "All I want is a chance to show you how good it can be between us."

The warm blue eyes were amused and beguiling, the voice a husky caress. His presence was a sweet irritant to her senses and she might have been overcome by it in another man, one whose face did not appear in page after magazine page in the company of some of the world's most beautiful women. She hoped that, at age twenty-four, she had a reasonable amount of self-confidence, but it stopped far short of classifying herself in their league. Her assess-

ment of his motives varied with what Renee called Kathy's
D.P.I. (Daily Paranoia Index). On days with a particularly
high D.P.I., she found herself contemplating such theories
as the one that the man wanted her to help him win some
little known title in the *Book of World Records*—Most
Women Seduced—or Renee's favorite, that Stratton was
having some kind of a mental breakdown brought on by
overwork, and that his relatives would someday use his
interest in Kathy to have him declared legally incompetent.
He was not the kind of man anyone could figure out overnight.

Kathy put her hands on his wrists to drag his palms away
from her, but he had begun to move his thumbs in a slow
rotation over the slope of her cheekbone, barely skimming
the nerve-enriched surfaces underneath her eyes. New record: greatest physical response from a woman with the
least effort. Some people seem to be born with a special
kind of magic, and Neil Stratton was one of them. She knew
she was staring at him in a bedazzled way as she whispered,
"Why me?"

"I wanted a lady who knows the score of *Camelot* by
heart, and Julie Andrews wouldn't give me a tumble."

"Vanessa Redgrave." In spite of herself, she could feel
her ache to answer his grin. "And add to that my invaluable
ability to replace your guitar pegs."

He was holding her so gently, and his eyes were so soft,
that she could almost taste the deep sweetness of the kiss
she knew he would offer her. It took every ounce of her
sense of purpose to drag herself out of his grip and say in
a level if slightly breathless voice, *"Somehow* you've
changed the subject. The vent fan—"

"Is not worth fighting about. As much as I admire the
psychic energy it has to take for you to say 'vent fan' as
though it was a mail-order marital aid—"

"I do not!"

"—there's a limit to the amount of time I can stay interested in that godforsaken slew of metal scraps. Since you
seem to think that buying you hardware will compromise
your honor, from now on I'll stick to candy and flowers.
Alright?"

"You," said Kathy, "had better stop talking to me as if
you think I'm some kind of hangover from the nineteenth

century. I may not live in Los Angeles or New York, but
that doesn't mean that— Drat you, Stratton, quit laughing
at me!"

"How can I help it? You're so damned earnest. Come
here."

Kathy heard herself utter a protesting squeak as he pulled
her to the carpeted floor. Muttering sharp little exclamations
like "Help!" and "What are you doing?" she was placed
firmly in a sitting position while he knelt behind her and
began to work his hands over her shoulders with short, easy
strokes.

She wasn't sure what it said about her state of mind, but
it took her fully thirty seconds to realize that all he meant
to do was to give her a back massage. In another thirty
seconds she realized it was a darn good one at that.

The rhythm of his hands swayed her body, brushing the
back of her thighs against the furred carpeting beneath her.
Moodily, not fighting him or herself, she stared between
her crossed ankles at the carpet between her parted knees
that held the swirling gold waves of her hair.

"Lady, you really need this," he said. His touch, precise
and luxurious, had begun to ease the tension from her muscles, flooding her raw nerves with a warm bath of sensation.

"My, you're good at this," she murmured, in a tone that
startled her with its languor and irrepressible note of sus-
picion.

"Don't make that sound so sinister." His voice smiled.
Gently, his fingers spread her hair, and her breasts tingled
at the delicate brush of his lips over the uncovered flesh of
her nape. As his thumbs worked into the knotted muscles
at the base of her neck, he said, "I ought to know how. I've
had it done to me enough times."

"Really?" she asked coldly. There was a single-beat
pause while she tried and failed to quell all interest in the
subject. Then, "Oh, all right. By whom?"

"Adolph. He's a big beefy guy in a white coat at my
health club. Lie down on your front and I'll give you the
full treatment."

"Thanks, but I think I'll pass."

Lightly, teasingly, he said, "I can make a new woman
out of you, Kathy Carter."

She was about to retort that *that* was what she was worried about, when the heel of his hand began to rotate slowly over her upper vertebrae. Some peculiar quirk of chemistry made every tissue in her being soften and blur like rippling velvet at his motion. Her spine seemed to slip apart and separate into jellied fragments. The soft utterance from her throat might almost have been a pleasure purr. His hands on her shoulders pressed her backward until she lay across his knees, limp as a wilted daisy.

"I'll have to remember," he said, scanning her with playful objectivity, "that you're a pushover for a good massage."

With care, his lips found hers, testing the pliant surface, skimming the arch of her lower lip. His mouth covered hers in an expanding kiss with a pressure that was heady and liquid as his tongue entered her. Moaning, she pressed herself more deeply into his kiss, her fingers spreading to feel the body contours that lay beneath his shirt.

His breath warmed her lips as he whispered, "I want to make love to you, Kathy."

Kathy's eyes fluttered open. Looking helplessly into the brimming affection in his expression, she tried to collect her scattered senses. At last she said, "Here? Is that a joke?"

Stratton's eyes sparkled with laughter. "I must have a wilder reputation than I realized. Darlin', if you're interested enough to think it over, maybe I did mean here . . ."

A sudden heavy vibration reached them. A large object in the studio had tumbled over. She dragged herself out of the rock star's arms, covering her tangled emotions with manufactured concern.

"*Now* what?" Kathy groaned.

"Someone is none-too-gently moving a speaker, I think." Stratton stretched a hand behind him and pressed the round knob of the dimmer switch. Misty artificial light swept from the ceiling lamp. For a moment he studied her silently as though he were searching through the emotional litter that lay beneath her feigned poise. Then he offered her his hand. "Shall we go back to the studio? And don't worry about Eric. If he gives you any more trouble, you and I are going to feed him an amplifier piece by piece."

5

THE SKY WAS a dark gleaming indigo feathered with opalescent clouds as Kathy folded herself, that evening, into the bucket seat of a black Ferrari next to Neil. Luxury. She warned herself not to get too used to it. Kathy didn't know how it might be in other parts of the country, but in small Wisconsin towns accepting a lift from someone who drove a Ferrari made her about as conspicuous as riding home in a derby hat on wheels. Townspeople were out-of-doors enjoying the pleasant evening, sitting on lawn chairs in their driveways or on porch swings, and Kathy found herself sliding as low as the seatbelt would allow. Much good it would do. All one thousand, two hundred and ninety-six of the town residents knew by now that she was "seeing" Neil Stratton.

"Nice car," she said, in a try at sophisticated understatement. "Is it yours?"

"No. Borrowed again. I don't like it. The clutch is a little stiff."

She looked around incredulously at the cinnamon leather upholstery, the walnut-paneled dash, the lush carpet that looked like it had been cut fresh from the bolt, the four-

speaker sound system. Kathy wondered briefly what kind
of car Stratton considered good enough to own.

"The clutch is a little stiff?" she repeated.

"Yeah," he said. "Car makes ice, though." He pushed
a button and Kathy jumped as a little portable bar fell out
of the dash in front of her, gushing crushed ice into a Steuben
glass tumbler.

"That's amazing," she said. "Do you ever use it?"

"No," he said. "Only by accident. When it rained on the
way up, I tried to put on the windshield wipers, but the bar
popped open and spat ice at me. Don't drink it. The ice
tastes like antifreeze."

Kathy cautiously sniffed the glass and decided he was
right. "What else does the car do?"

"You've noticed I don't use the horn. It plays 'O Solo
Mio.' The seats recline. I could lay you back faster than
you could say 'On Wisconsin'." He turned the corner from
the highway onto Broad Street and headed for the shop.

"If you turn right here and go into the alley behind the
shop, we could go in the back way," she suggested. He
gave her a smile and did it. Kathy felt proud of Apple Grove;
even the backs of the stores were kept painted. She had
done her turn with the brush; and the alley was free of
potholes. An undeveloped field full of wildflowers and
waving alfalfa broke the line of houses in back of the stores
in the next block, and their sharp scent permeated the breeze
that washed into the car through the open windows. Neil
shut off the engine and turned to her.

"Can I demonstrate the reclining seat now?" he asked.

"No, thanks," she said. "The ice was enough excitement
for one night."

His hand, hazel-complected and patterned with soft
brown hair, had come to rest on the leather-wrapped steering
wheel as he gazed at her with those daylight blue eyes.
There was nothing intense about his expression; it suggested
friendship and a certain easygoing amusement. Don't ask
him to come in, Kathy Carter. Don't ask him to come in.
Danger.

Kathy heard her voice say hesitantly, "I suppose the least
I can do is ask if you'd like to come in for some coffee?"
Mayday. Mayday. Brain malfunction. All barriers left intact
report immediately to the frontal lobe. Bring pictures of

Stratton's discarded love interests. Bring reminders of Kathy Carter's soppy-soft heart that's going to get blistered in any relationship where the male party doesn't include love and commitment in the bargain. Kathy did not consider herself to be a good-time girl. To Neil, whose expression had undergone a subtle change, she said, "I wish you wouldn't look at me like that."

"I'm sorry," he said, getting out of the car and coming around to open her door. "On my way upstairs, I'll try to change my look."

As they stepped into the back room of the shop, Kathy saw a giant black object that hadn't been there when she'd left at noon. "What in blazes is that?" she said, and switched on the light. "Oh, my. Another tuba."

Neil walked over to the instrument, which lay in its monstrous open case, its enormous bell yawning wide. There was a note tied to the mouthpiece. He read, "Hi! I'm Tubby the Tuba. Lubricate my valves."

"My sister," said Kathy. "She's the kind who can't resist writing 'wash me' with her finger on the back of a dirty car."

He followed her up the stairs and into the apartment. She had left the window open. The curtain belled and flattened with the movement of the evening air. She turned on the lamp at the end of her couch and a big brown moth came to bat against the screen. From out in the country, near the Black Bridge, came the long, high moan of a train whistle. She looked at Neil at the sound and smiled in spite of herself.

"The Thursday train!" he said. "It's two days late." He walked into the apartment after her with a familiarity that reminded her he had already been in it—when he had run upstairs to get her a sweater before he took her out on the day of their first meeting. It had been chilly then at night. It wasn't chilly now. She led him through the living room, past the overstuffed couch with its lace antimacassar and across the old Persian carpet that had been her mother's. She wondered what he thought of her house, with its old iron tongue-and-groove latches on the doors and its uneven hardwood floors. Stopping before the spinet piano where her Beatles songbook was open to "Yesterday," he touched the melody out of the keys with easy familiarity, but stopped in the middle and switched into a jaunty, multi-rhythmic tune that he played as though he had suddenly grown ten extra fingers. It created an image in her mind of sophisticated ladies and gents stepping out in a fast-paced, classy urban setting.

"'Satin Doll'," she said, remembering the tune. He was much better than she was—of course; had she expected otherwise?—with a more controlled touch and a finer, more subtle sense of rhythm. She felt a sudden flash of insecurity, vulnerability . . . inferiority. It had been hanging in the background since she had first seen him talking with the Fire-crackers. Suddenly, as though he sensed her feelings, his fingers lifted from the keyboard. Smiling wryly, he captured her gaze and said, with a slightly lifted brow, "Enough of that. Coffee."

She had a friendly kitchen, warm and whimsical. Renee had painted a bright yellow sun on one wall, with pretty yellow rays reaching up the wall and halfway across the ceiling. Three cuckoo clocks hung in a V formation on the far wall, their hands carefully adjusted so they would all go into action at once. All the clocks were busy, announcing that it was eight o'clock, each to its own routine. The toaster sat under its quilted cover shaped like a sleeping cat with a long stuffed tail on a bright yellow tray under the ruffled eyelet curtains. The white refrigerator held up a colorful flock of felt butterfly magnets made by one of her piano students.

Neil rinsed and filled her coffeepot as Kathy coaxed a flame from a burner on her aged gas range, and then walked around the kitchen, touching little things that interested him, running his sensitive fingers over the golden grain of her antique oak kitchen table, asking her light questions about things he saw, about her family. He mentioned her father.

Late in the afternoon, Kathy's father had stopped by Audio Art on an embarrassingly slim pretext, his obvious intent to meet the dashing out-of-town fellow who was spending time with his younger daughter. Apparently, Neil had never faced an interview with the father of one of his ladies, because he had seemed to find a quaint and charming novelty in the situation. Within ten minutes, Neil Stratton had had her father completely snowed.

"My father's a saint," Kathy said glumly.

"How was it, growing up with a saintly father?"

"Well...It made Renee into kind of a rebel," Kathy said.

"But not you?"

"No," she admitted. "I couldn't see any point in rebelling. Daddy never noticed when we did anything bad. Once, when my sister was fifteen, he came home early from a prayer meeting and caught Renee and her friends drinking beer in our basement. Did he get mad? No. He gave them a beatific smile and said how happy he was that they'd gotten interested in collecting aluminum cans for recycling and, before any of them knew what was happening, he had them traipsing all over town collecting cans to raise money for new choir robes." The burner went out. Relighting it with an oversized wooden match, she said, "You were a big hit with him. You've been a big hit with *everyone.*"

Responding only to the first part of her observation, he said, "I have the feeling that it would be hard not to be a hit with your father."

"True. The man has no discrimination. He's fond of all creatures, be they kids, adults, fish, fowl, or rabid coyotes. Case in point: Freddie and the Firecrackers. Neil, there's something I haven't said that I should have, and that's, thank you for the things you've done for the boys. I still can't believe the graceful way you walked Eric away from his anger at you...You've worked a small miracle."

"It was a Band-Aid, Kathy. Eric's got a lot of problems, and none of them are going to go away overnight. Still, with enough of the right kind of attention..." Neil was rearranging the refrigerator butterflies into the shape of a heart. "The three of them are lucky to have you. You're a remarkable woman."

The unexpected compliment cast her into witless confusion. Cautiously, trying not to give away too much of her rattling disquiet, she said, "I may choke on admitting this, but you're much better with them than I am. You have a way of getting them to go along with new things."

"Typical musicians," Neil said easily. "I've had to learn to get along with bigger egos than theirs. As long as you let them know you understand what they're trying to get across, the situation usually stays within reason."

But Kathy was disconcerted to realize that she had hardly heard what he said. An oddly foolish and uncontrollable

urge had led her helpless gaze down his neck and into the
open point of his shirt, where the cozy kitchen lamp etched
a V of light-gilded male flesh. No matter how hard she tried
to drag her gaze to his eyes, her stare drifted back to his
chest, or to his lips, or to the soft sheen of his hair. He was
about four feet from her . . . what was the matter with her,
counting the feet that separated them! And, to her shame,
she had almost forgotten what he was talking to her about.

"So," she said, willing away her awareness of him as
a man, "you mentioned to my father that you've been in
Chicago since early this morning. An interview, he said.
What interview in this neck of the woods?"

"A syndicated talk show."

"No kidding? *The* syndicated talk show?" How queer
and unlike her her voice was starting to sound. "You're
going to be on television. When can I turn you on? No! I
mean . . . I mean . . ." The only avenue open was to turn
quickly away from his subtle smile, to pretend to be busy
in the cabinet.

After a minute, she heard his voice behind her. "I like
your coffee cups. It's been a long time since I've drunk out
of anything with Mickey Mouse on it. But are there going
to be more than two of us?"

Kathy looked down at the long row of mugs she had just
unloaded on the counter before her. Obviously, she was
losing her mind. With dismay, she said, "No, of course not.
I'll put them back up again."

She lifted her arms to put the mugs away and suddenly
felt his hands warm on her waist. The surprise, and, yes,
the inadvertent thrill made her pause and close her eyes,
and his hands began a slow, comfortable up-and-down motion on her sides, palms flat, fingers spread on her rib cage,
his fingertips barely skimming her midriff. She gently and
deliberately set the cups down and gripped the edge of the
shelf to steady herself against the tremor which ran through
her at his touch. He felt her tension, and placed his lips in
her hair next to her ear.

"Easy, Kathy—it's all right." His voice was a husky,
smokily sensual rasp. She heard it through a mist of desire,
and the feeling she had of wanting him to lift his fingertips
to the tips of her breasts was so strong that dizziness overtook
her and she had to lean her head against the smooth wood

of the cabinet. His hands skimmed with such adeptness, such sureness, over the fabric of her fitted knit t-shirt that they might have been caressing her naked skin. She felt her nipples swelling urgently against the cloth, and the smooth, rounded edge of the hardwood countertop against her thighs made her want him to press her to his hard body, to mold her into him.

"Neil." She whispered his name.

"Mmm?" His lips were still in her hair, tugging on her earlobe. "Tell me what you want, Kathy."

"Neil, I..." She had never, in her limited experience with men, heard that request. Tell me what you want, he had said. "Neil, I... touch me. Touch me." His hands traveled with light, steady friction over her ribs until the undercurve of her breasts rested on his spread palms, and her breasts felt heavy and throbbed for his touch. And the next husky whisper was her own. "Please." His hands cradled softly upward, until the tips of her breasts were cupped warmly in his palms, his fingers gently kneading the aching flesh. Her long, slow respiration pressed her softness deeply into his hands. Never, never had it been like this for her. His forefingers lifted to circle and probe over the fabric covering her nipples.

"Is that what you wanted?" he asked softly.

Her lips were slightly parted, her breath quickening, her insides a turmoil of voluptuous sensations, but she spoke when his hands slipped away. "Don't stop," she said in a whisper. But he was only reaching to turn off the overhead light, leaving on only the small Tiffany lamp on the telephone stand, and touched off the burner under the coffee. And then his warmth was behind her again, and she felt, with a mixture of desire and excited apprehension, his thumbs hooking into the straps of her shirt and pulling them down over her gracefully rounded shoulders.

"Lower your arms, darlin'," he murmured, and she did, and he slowly slipped the straps down her bare arms. The fabric tugged a little over her standing nipples before it fell free down around her waist, and he caressed the plane of her stomach with one hand as, with the other, he lifted her thick light hair from her neck and kissed the sloping hollow between her neck and shoulder. And then he lifted his hands once again, and she gasped at the sensation of the flesh-on-flesh contact, at the arousing, erotic massage of the sides of his thumbs across the underside of her breast tips. Her hands flat on the counter in front of her, the fingers spread for support, she began unconsciously to make subtle yearning motions with her hips, moaning as he pressed himself against her from behind.

"Kathy, you're so beautiful." He slipped his hands down her arms and interlaced his fingers with hers, slowly turning her to face him, pulling her hands up and back, settling them behind his neck. She lifted her chin, turning her head, her eyes closed in rapt absorption in the pleasure of his circling hands and the burning trail of his lips on the side of her neck across her jaw, finally, after what seemed to her like a pleasurable eternity, reaching her waiting mouth. Their lips met and parted and met once again in a deep, clinging kiss, his tongue gently circling the sensitive skin on the inside of her lips. When the kiss was over, she gazed up at him, seeing through her desire-misted vision the tenderness in his eyes as his fingers touched the fair skin of her neck where her pulse beat so rapidly.

There was no need for words now; they were communicating through gesture. He turned her to him, his hands on her shoulders, and their lips met again, exploring, liquid, desirous. Her hair was streaming down her back, and he filled his hands with it as though he were touching a precious mass of gold. Her lips blindly searched his as his hands traveled down her back, and he pressed her into him, then, with a single liberating motion, he unsnapped her jeans and moved his hands around her to slip them onto the firm, muscular swelling of her bottom under her jeans. Her breath was coming in long, deep waves, slow and natural, enjoying the present moment, waiting heedlessly for the next. His mouth moved slowly down over her fluted collarbone, and in a smooth, powerful motion he lifted her onto the counter. Her breathing increased in depth and speed as his lips and tongue worked on the pink tips of her breasts and then moved lower, and her head was bowed over him, her hair falling onto him, as he ran his tongue over the subtle swell of her lower belly, his hands kneading her in slow, sensual pulses.

"Neil . . ." she moaned.

"Let's go to bed—" his voice was a sensual rasp—"and

be good to each other." He lifted her, his strong arms around her back and under her knees, and she leaned her head back onto his shoulder, feeling light and dreamy as he carried her. Her eyes fluttered open and looked at him in wonderment, glorying in the colors of him. If he opened his arms, she would surely float on air. She felt newborn into an amniotic dimension of blurred light and flying sensation. It had been so different before, with David...

With David. Over the rise of Neil's shoulder, her gaze caught the wood-framed color photograph of herself and David on the low table beneath the bedroom window. In wonderful tenderness, Neil bent to lay her on the bed where she had slept in David's arms, where on that first difficult night of marriage she had tried so hard to find joy in the awkward thing that love had seemed...Don't think about it. David. David, a gray moon-bright profile, ruffling her hair with a big hand and saying, "Hey, K.C. It's nothing to cry over. So we weren't the last of the red hot lovers. Neither of us have had any experience with this stuff before, and it's gonna take us a while..." Don't think about it! Don't think about the while that had never ended. Don't think about unhealed regrets. Don't...

"Don't!" She said the word aloud. Nausea and the remnant feeling of a cold sweat congealed in her senses as she repeated, "Don't...don't."

Neil responded immediately, setting her swiftly, carefully on the floor, his hands supporting her as she found her balance. David's face remained before her, a faint, blurred image, and for a moment her throat was so tight that she couldn't swallow. A feeling that she was strangling began to grow in her. Through the haze of emotion and the accusing mirage of her lost love, she saw Neil Stratton raise his hand and felt the light pressure of his fingers on her cheek. The sensation was clean and soothing.

"What happened?" he asked.

Something kept her from being able to answer him, or face his searching gaze. She felt more than saw his eyes leave hers to stray to the low table, briefly examining the photograph, coming back to her. His breathing was controlled, faintly rapid. His touch on her skin was steady and she could feel the roughness of his fingertips, the legacy of years spent pounding steel guitar strings.

"What made the lady change her mind?" he asked.

"It was happening too quickly." She could barely manage the words.

"Sometimes," he said quietly, "that's the way it happens."

Teetering numbly over pools of guilt, confusion, and desire, Kathy felt herself leap blindly away from them and into anger. If she was enraged with anyone, it was herself, yet she heard her voice whispering, "Does it? I wouldn't know. Is that something you've discovered in your vast experience?"

He was silent for a moment, gazing down at her through dark-lashed eyes, the drooping lids half-concealing the blue fire below. He made no attempt to conceal his emotions, but that made them no easier for her to read. His expression might have shown anything from hurt to disgust, or even a kind of simple curiosity about her sudden and inexplicable rebuff.

Abruptly, he turned and walked to the window. Parting the ruffled curtain, he bent to look out, seemingly to breathe the fresh night air. She awkwardly pulled her top up; the large snap on her jeans suddenly seemed microscopically tiny. He put his palms on the sill and straightened his arms; she could see the muscles in his back flexing tensely.

"If my experience is a problem for you, we should talk about it," he said.

Her stomach twisted into a knot and she involuntarily placed her clenched fist there. Talking about Neil's ladies was more than she could handle. "What fun," she said tiredly. "Another time. Sit down. I'll bring coffee."

Retreating to the kitchen, she forced herself not to cry, because the sobs filling up her chest were loud, gulping ones. The last thing she wanted was for him to hear her cry. Her pride couldn't stand another buffet. For a fairly rational person, with what she had always considered to be a perfectly reasonable measure of self-control, it was getting harder and harder for her to understand why she was so vulnerable to Neil Stratton.

She did not believe herself to be a sensual person. Why could this near-stranger carry her toward rich, shining horizons when with David, the man she had loved all her life, the intimacies of married life had held no more erotic excitement than did pulling on warm woolens on a winter morning? A man she hardly knew had touched her, had run his hands over the most intimate and sensitive parts of her body. And it had felt so good, sweeter than the sweetest things in her life—sweeter than hearing an oriole's song on a summer meadow, sweeter than fresh-squeezed lemonade on a hot evening, better than the springtide of lilacs... She moved slowly and carefully while she brought the coffee, trying to regain her composure. She was beginning to realize with increasing force that she was in no position, emotionally or otherwise, to be involved with someone as worldly as he was. It amazed her still that he had even returned; and he was talking about being a part of her life. But her life was not ready for Neil Stratton.

She came out of the kitchen taking slow, steadying breaths, a mug of hot coffee in each hand. Neil was in her bedroom standing by the low table and holding her wedding picture, which he was studying with an intent objectivity.

Kathy and David. The photographer had posed them beside a stained-glass window and the light had been kind to him. He'd had classic good looks, but his rugged features usually photographed heavily and his short, conservative haircut often gave his face a severity that was absent in his character. Only a close friend could detect the slight puffiness from the cold he was getting over. She could remember her mother stuffing him with antihistamines at the reception. The diffuse light had flattered her own face as well as she gazed with porcelain vacancy through the folds of her grandmother's wedding veil, the red tea roses and baby's breath from her wreath nodding against her temples...

She lifted her gaze to Neil, watching him skim his forefinger slowly over David's face like a sightless person, even though he could feel only the flat, reflective surface of the glass. Neil, with his extraordinary force of personality, his vitality, his much-heralded sex appeal... Kathy experienced a flash of pure protectiveness toward David that was undiminished as Neil said, "He's dead?"

"Yes." Then, stiffly, "How did you know that?"

"If you'd divorced the guy, you wouldn't be likely to keep your wedding picture by your bed. And this—" he indicated the low table where small Wedgewood vases held twin arrangements of forget-me-nots—"is a shrine."

He might have read a grocery list with more sympathy. She had hardly expected reverence, but this offhand, almost callous appraisal was a shock.

"It's not a shrine." Her voice was tight and crisp. "That happens to be a good place to put flowers."

Stratton showed no reaction either to her words or to her hostility. Setting down the photograph, he took the coffee without touching her fingers, and gave her a smile that was tame and collected.

"If you have any other pictures," he said, "I'd like to see them."

She wanted to say no, but when she mentally rehearsed her refusal, it sounded too defensive. She already felt she had exposed much more of her vulnerability to him than she could stand. So she brought him her scrap book and sat on her Bentwood rocker watching Neil Stratton, idol of millions, as he perused her life, just as she had examined his in the glossy magazines in the Madison public library.

He opened to the first page, to an enlarged snapshot of herself and David as three-year-olds, when their mothers had dressed them as Raggedy Ann and Raggedy Andy for Halloween. Next year, on the facing page, they were Ma and Pa Kettle, with corncob pipes and a painted bleach bottle labeled "moonshine."

And then they were eight, at his grandfather's farm, straddling the bare back of old Clyde, the quarter horse, she in front, he with his arm protectively around her, both of them missing their front teeth. And the picture of them at church camp when they were eleven, taken by firelight with a flash; they were dressed as Indian brave and squaw for a skit. And then they were sixteen, homecoming king and queen in the convertible, holding umbrellas in the rain. Later, at the dance—with a pink carnation from her corsage pressed into the book beside the picture. David in his letter sweater, and then she in it, overwhelmed by the folds. The letter rested opposite, its bright fabric softened and fading.

Graduation. Off to college. Both had lived at home with their parents through the four years, driving the thirty miles to the state college branch every day together. Here was the picture Renee had taken on that day, their grins eager and touchingly naïve as they set out for their big adventure. By then, Neil Stratton's second album had gone platinum, and he was living in Paris with the heiress to a British automobile manufacturing fortune. Once, according to the magazine, they had rented a jet and flown to Iceland for lunch on the side of a volcano.

The scrapbook continued. David with the college team... more letters... clippings from the sports section of the college paper. A group photo from his year as president of his engineering fraternity. College graduation. Marriage. David's life—begun in black and white, ending in Kodacolor. The hunter-cum-conservationist who never took a shot unless he was sure of a clean kill. One of the last pictures was a blowup of David on one knee with his arms around Whiskey, his golden retriever. For a month after David was gone, Whiskey had lain pining by the front door, his eyes sorrowful, his wet nose between his paws. Old age, the young vet had said after Whiskey died peacefully in his sleep, but Kathy knew a broken heart when she saw one.

Neil leafed through the album, asking her to identify a person, a place, asking about the memorabilia pressed between the pages: the napkin from their graduation banquet, the ribbon from first prize in the sack race at the Sunday School picnic; all the rest of it.

And finally, on the last page, was David's obituary, clipped from the paper. "Ex-quarterback Platteville State Falls, Dies of Cerebral Hemmorhage During Freak Hunting Accident." Neil closed the book.

"So," he said. "Where do you save his old sweat socks?"

It took Kathy a moment or two to accept that he'd really said it. She stood up, and in a voice that trembled, said, "I think you'd better leave."

"I will. Shortly." He had stood also, and as she watched in angry confusion, he opened her scrapbook and removed the photograph of David on his knee beside Whiskey. From the low table beside her bedroom window, he picked up her wedding picture, withdrew that photograph from the frame, and inserted the one of David and his dog.

"I don't know why you think you belong with him in that touching memorial display," Neil said. He brought her wedding picture back to the scrapbook, attaching it to the blank page. "He's dead. You're not." He set the framed picture of David and Whiskey on her bureau. Distress and some subliminal instinct of shock had made her grab up her scrapbook and hold it to her body in both hands. She loosened one hand briefly to yank open her door.

"You aren't used to hearing the word 'no', are you?" she choked out furiously.

Neil stopped and faced her. The mesmeric blue eyes held her in a thick embrace as he crossed the Persian carpet to her. With unwilling fascination, she followed the spare, graceful motion of his body as he took the scrapbook from her, crossed back to the bed, dragged back the bedclothes, and tossed the scrapbook on the cornflower-and-white patterned sheets.

"Sleep with it," he said. And left.

6

RENEE STOOD BY Kathy's workbench, her chin propped in a fist. "One of the Collins kids brought this in," she said, freeing her hand to give Kathy a forlorn-looking brass trumpet. "He said it had an air leak."

"Oh, did he now?" said Kathy, putting the trumpet to her lips. She blew a scale. "He's not kidding it's got an air leak. Water key, I think." Reaching down, Kathy flicked on the leaklight with her thumb and threaded it into the horn. "Gad, Miss Frobisher," she said in her best bad British accent, "there are things growing in here. It looks like the forest floor of the Zambezi Basin."

"Bad, is it?" queried her sister.

"The worst. We could stock a pharmaceutical company on the mold alone." She put down the trumpet and brushed distractedly at the felt bits that clung to the blue cuffs of her shorts, the residue of her late morning's work cutting flute pads. "Do ring the maid, Frobisher, and tell her we're ready to take tay."

"The maid," said Renee with a quirky grin, "will be delighted. She was about to perish from thirst." Dragging a bright plaid thermos from a needlepoint carryall, she poured a plastic cupful of iced tea for Kathy and one for herself, and then came to sprawl lazily in the antique desk chair in the corner, gazing thoughtfully at Kathy, who was sitting with her shoulders slumped, staring dejectedly at her own reflection in the clear liquid.

Outside, filmy gray clouds sprinkled rain on the street and on the green striped canvas awning suspended above the plate-glass shop window. Water chimed and gurgled through the downspouts.

Kathy looked outside. "It's letting up," she said, straightening her back, stretching, and rubbing her neck.

"So it is." Renee watched the ice clink in her glass. "You know," she said slowly, "it's a good thing it happened in your kitchen and not in mine."

"What do you mean? Why?"

"Because," Renee said, "you're so tidy. If a man lifted me up on my kitchen counter and started to make love to me, I'd come down with orange juice rings on my rear end. Did you hear what Daddy said about Neil?"

"That he was a nice boy?" Kathy buried her nose in the red thermos cup.

"Not exactly," Renee said, crunching an ice chip. "He said, 'You can see why they made that young man a star.' Anyway, you seem better today, Kath."

Getting down from her stool, Kathy stretched again, extending the pull throughout her body, closing her eyes. "I've decided that three days is enough to mope about a fight with any man, star or no."

"He hasn't called?" Renee asked, gently.

Kathy opened her eyes. "No." She wandered around the counter, her face to the shop window. "He knows better. And why should he? He's made it clear he thinks I'm a neurotic widow hooked on some treadmill of self-denial."

There was a short pause before Renee said, "Are you?"

"I don't know." Kathy's eyes stung with the syrupy weight of gathering moisture. "Probably. Neurotic? After a couple of months of Stratton, neurotic is a moderate word for what I am. One minute of Stratton is like an hour in a Cuisinart. Kathy Carter emerges chopped, shredded, and diced. No, thanks. No more." Going back around the desk, Kathy stared blankly downward, and felt the hushed movement of warm air as Renee came to her side and put a slim arm around her shoulders. Kathy let her head droop against her sister's offered shoulder and blinked hard as Renee rocked her slowly back and forth.

"Small-town girl meets famous musician," Renee said. "Sounds like a fairy tale."

"It sounds," Kathy said tersely, "like a strange French art film. You don't have to see his diploma to know that Stratton got his Ph.D. in Arrogance." She drew herself upright, giving her sister a rueful grin as she handed her a cup and picked up her own.

"Tea and sympathy," Kathy murmured. Seeing that Renee was looking beyond, out the shop window, she turned her head with slight interest and saw that a white van with green trim and a winged florist's Mercury figure had pulled up outside the shop.

"Flowers?" said Kathy, her interest perking up. "Are you expecting anything, Renee? What type of—oh!"

The uniformed delivery man pushed open the door with his foot. He was holding a huge crystal vase full of long-stemmed red and white roses mingled with lush green ferns. "Kathy Carter?"

"Yes?"

He set his burden on the counter and smiled. "These are for you."

"Oh, Kathy, they're beautiful!" exclaimed Renee. Kathy had left her chair and stood staring at the beautiful bouquet, mustering her courage, quelling the trembling in her fingers enough to be able to tear open the message which accompanied them.

"'When we kiss,'" she read, "'this is what I see. Neil.'" Laughing a little, she showed the card to Renee and circled the flowers with her palms, bringing the lovely scented petals to her face and breathing deeply in.

"Where should I put the rest of them, ma'am?" asked the delivery man.

"The rest of them?" Kathy said blankly.

"Yes, ma'am," he said, tilting back his hat, his face splitting into a homely grin. "Somebody sure likes you, ma'am. There's plenty more where that came from."

There were, to be precise, one hundred and ninety-eight dozen more roses. Fragrant nodding blossoms spread an avalanche of scent and color in bowery drifts that filled every corner of her shop forty-five minutes later. A laughing, pointing, exclaiming crowd gathered on the drying pavement beyond. Someone fetched Kathy's father from where he had been painting one of the rooms in the church basement and brought Renee's husband Jack from his office at the implement factory, but it was Mavis from the Apple Grove *Republican* who took the picture of Kathy alone amidst the floor of living blossoms. Kathy tried to find good homes for the flowers. Her father was delighted to call in the Ladies' Aid, who arrived like a cavalry charge in their station wagons and recreational vehicles to distribute the roses to nursing homes and hospitals all over the county. If only it had been as easy to get rid of the press.

By one of those strange quirks of fate, it was the sort of day that gives nightmares to news editors. Nothing happened. No prominent people died. There were no catastrophic natural disasters. The Supreme Court handed down no momentous decisions. So when the wire services picked up the story of a young Wisconsin widow beseiged by $4,800 (some estimates went as high as $7,000) worth of roses from rock star Neil Stratton, the photograph Mavis took with her serviceable box camera ended up on pages one or two of newspapers all over the nation.

On the afternoon of the morning Mavis's picture was bought by the wire services, Kathy got her first phone call— a woman reporter from the popular magazine *Metro Gal*, based in New York, wanting to do a human-interest feature on what it was like to be the girlfriend of a famous rock star, complete with a fashion layout of Kathy wearing designer apparel which she couldn't have afforded had she saved her profits for two years.

Bright and early the next morning, she got a phone call from old Mrs. Hazelhurst, whose house backed the alley across from the shop. A photographer from a popular weekly supermarket tabloid had offered her a hundred dollars for permission to sit on the roof of her back porch to take snapshots of Kathy coming and going in the alley.

"Mrs. Hazelhurst, if he's foolish enough to pay you that much money to sit on your roof, if I were you, I'd take it," Kathy said.

Forewarned, she used the front door all day. Then that evening at a family picnic in Renee's back yard, Kathy caught an AP stringer skulking in the shrubbery after she saw her eight-year-old niece handing a hot dog into the lilac bushes.

Bad went to worse the next morning as Kathy sat at her workbench in the shop sorting through her mail, and found a letter addressed to her from the nationally known magazine that had made "centerfold" a household word. Inside they offered her more than just a good subscription rate.

The phone, swathed in its masking tape repair made on the day of the vent fan, made an irritable whirr. She perched on the edge of her desk and picked up the receiver.

"Kathy Carter's Instrument Repair."

"Kathy, this is Neil." Through the twanging reverb of a long-distance line came the voice of a man who caused thousands across the world every day to lay down their hard-earned cash for a plastic disc with his voice grooved into it. "Are you all right?"

Words could not convey the depths of her emotion. She had to settle for tone of voice.

"Oh, I'm fine, Neil, fine. Do you know what I have sitting in front of me? A letter. Do you know who sent it to me? The company that brought girlie magazines out of the plain brown wrapper. You know, the one everyone says they read for the articles? It seems they're doing an article on groupies—and guess who they want to audition for their centerfold?"

"Love, I'm sorry." His voice was soft.

"Why be sorry, Mr. Stratton? You said you were going to take care of me. Look at the wonderful door that's opened for me! Why, it could be the start of a whole new career!"

"Honey, listen to me . . ."

"Don't 'honey' me. There's a man sitting on the roof across the alley who takes pictures of me every time I stick my head out. *Metro Gal* wants me to model lingerie. Next time, Mr. Stratton, save your flamboyant gestures for the stage." She hung up. The phone rang again almost immediately. She snatched at it.

"Apparently I haven't made myself clear," she continued. "I'm not your plaything. I don't know if what you're doing is some sort of subtle revenge on me for refusing to go to bed with you, or if you simply have a warped sense of humor. But I don't enjoy being made infamous. If you have anything else to say, say it, because I want to get off the phone."

"Mrs. Carter, this is Eric Carpenter," came a deadpan voice. "Sorry. I'll call you back later."

Renee's strongly stated opinion was that Kathy had no business being angry with a man who had sent her two hundred dozen roses. And, in her weakest moments, Kathy couldn't fight off the germ of regret that she hadn't listened to Neil's explanation over the telephone, or read even one of the two letters from him that she'd returned unopened. Honest self-evaluation warned her that she might be doing more than outwardly resisting the relationship. She might be trying to sabotage it. There was, for example, the way she had handled her change of heart the evening he had come so close to making love to her in her apartment. Granted, there were a lot of reasons for her to have been emotional and confused, but even so, she could have been less flippant in her manner and more communicative. Any way she examined it, her own behavior that night was nothing she could look on with pride.

Her own conduct aside, she was no closer than she'd ever been to being able to adjust to Neil's interest, though she was having to throw up bigger and bigger barricades to resist it. She couldn't accustom herself to the risks of the relationship, to the eccentricities imposed by his prominence and his lifestyle, to his readiness to plunge her into an uncommitted love affair. Neil Stratton's greatest crime was that she needed him too much, and in the three weeks that followed, she had more time than she wanted to find out just how true that was.

She learned from Mike that Neil was in New York, wrapped up in his own recording work. He kept in touch with Freddie and the Firecrackers, calling them occasionally at the school, giving them support and advice, but toward the end of July even the calls had become less frequent.

The situation was becoming desperate. The Firecrackers were scheduled to play at the county fair the last week in August, and the tape was to have been finished and pressed into records by then for sale after their concert, and it didn't look like they would be ready. Kathy did her best to keep the boys at work during their scheduled studio time, but no

one's heart was in it, her own included. Neil had jokingly
told her that he intended to make her dependent on him, but
the cruel truth was that he had done it.

And not only was she dependent on him, so were the
kids. They weren't ready to work on their own. His help
had whetted their taste for more sophisticated achievements
that they had only a glimmer of how to execute without
him. His help had been immeasurable, but in his absence
they were in worse shape than ever. For one thing, Fritz
Waller had gotten into the habit of staying to watch them
work, and in the weeks preceding, Neil's live-wire charisma
had been the catalyst that made them all seem like one big
happy family. One session without him had shot that comfortable illusion. Inside of ten minutes, Fritz and the Firecrackers were at each other's throats, and by the time Kathy's father came to drive the boys back to school, Kathy
was ready to go home to warm milk, a hot bath, an aspirin,
and bed.

Only two things had appreciably improved as a result of
Neil's intervention in their lives—their sound (though what
good did it do if they didn't have the expertise to capture
it properly on tape?) and the way Eric treated Kathy. But
with each passing session, and each day of mounting frustration, they were all increasingly eager to squabble.

Things came to a head late one afternoon while she was
off picking up hamburgers for them on her bike. She walked
back into Fritz's store with a shopping bag full of hot sandwiches and found catastrophe. By a freak accident in the
studio Fritz had erased the Firecrackers' master tape and,
with it, three months of sweat and toil. Eric, in a blind fit
of temper at the loss, had shoved his fist through the studio
window.

Kathy heard the glass shatter as she was running the
gauntlet of dishwashers. Like a movie reel spun too quickly,
she remembered for long after the blood hiccuping from an
artery in Eric's forearm and the blurred hysteria of a ride
to the hospital in Fritz Waller's van, trying to recall first
aid rules about tourniquets and pressure points and com-
forting Eric, who was repeating hazy apologies for the mess,
the trouble, and the blood that was beginning to spread dark
carnations of color over Kathy's white blouse and shorts.

At the hospital she filled out admission forms with unsteady fingers, and explained what had happened to her father when he arrived, and to the social worker from Walworth, and finally to Renee and Jack. They made it to the hospital just as a nurse brought them the news that Eric had come successfully through the surgery and that the doctor would be out in a few minutes to speak with them. A lady of resource under any and all situations, her sister had even thought to bring Kathy a change of clothes.

The nurse took Kathy to one of the vacant rooms on the maternity floor, where she could shower and change. Kathy waited, after she finished, until Eric was awake enough for a quick, quiet visit from her. Lavender twilight had settled on the parking lot as she left the hospital with Jack and Renee and she put up no more than a token resistance when they announced they were going to take her out to dinner and after that bring her home to spend the night with them.

It was quite late when Jack turned his Cadillac into their driveway. Kathy could see the errant flicker behind the filmy window curtains that meant the babysitter was watching television. Late-night television reminded her of insomnia, and insomnia reminded her in a way she couldn't calculate of Neil Stratton. The unsettled feelings made her restless and she decided that it might relax her to take a short stroll to the park before going to bed.

Moonlight tipped rooftops and silver-patched the trees over her head as she walked. A warm wind pressed the silk of her halter dress sensuously against her legs and moved like a moist breath on her bare shoulders. Crickets yodeled from the bushes beneath the blackened windows of the houses she passed. Locusts trilled.

The clear hoot of a hunting owl came from behind her, and the magnificent bird floated down the middle of the street like a fleeting thought. The sky was a deep, star-dusted black. It was all safe and familiar to Kathy, and she was glad she had stayed in Apple Grove instead of going to Milwaukee or Chicago like so many of her high school classmates had done.

The park was on the north edge of town, six blocks away, and sometimes deer would come there. Here, all was quiet, and peaceful. The swings moved back and forth in the breeze.

A sandstone bandstand filled the center of the park, used

since the Civil War for Saturday night concerts. Kathy walked once around it, trailing her fingers along the cold, rough surface, singing softly, and then climbed the flight of four steps and sat on the stone railing, swinging her legs, plucking a leaf from the overgrown snowball bush that grew nearby, and stroking it idly against the railing as she sang.

A movement from the steps, a slanting shadow, made her look up.

"Lovely voice. Lovely woman."

The words hardly pierced her consciousness as she absorbed the impact of the speaker's identity. Neil. He stood ten feet away, watching her. One hand, bare under a rolled-up cuff, was resting on the balustrade beside hips that were casually encased in doeskin pants. A soft chambray shirt hugged his well-modeled upper body. The effect was of understated elegance that demanded good looks, money, and immutable self-confidence.

She had wondered many times since he left her after the angry night in her apartment how she would feel when she saw him again, yet she was still unprepared for the overriding power of her urge to walk into his arms. His eyes, lucid and engaging, offered her the embrace that he made no move to promote. She stood without moving, gazing back at him, shaking down the need that rose inside her like liquid in a thermometer shaft.

"Mike called me," he said.

"Oh?" It was amazing to hear her own voice invest so much hostility in the single syllable. "Are you going to see Eric?"

"I already have." There was a moment's pause. "Renee told me I could find you here," he added absently. "I'm sure you have a few choice things you'd like to say to me. I've come to listen."

Her tight grip on the stone railing had become painful. Kathy closed her eyes, trying to ease her breathing, fighting her wish to melt into him.

"Goodness," she said, to the night, the trees, and the wind. "What a lot of trouble. Why didn't you just stay in New York and use your imagination?" She had a sudden, intense sensation that he was about to touch her, and her eyes opened quickly under tense brows. But Neil was still standing where he had been by the balustrade. She inhaled

silently, and this time, said evenly, "You were right about
one thing. You said you'd make us dependent on Neil Stratton and, my, did you ever. It's a pity I didn't realize in the
beginning that if things didn't prosper between the two of
us, you were going to shed those three kids like rainwater
off a slicker."

"I haven't shed the kids," he said. "My interest in them
has nothing to do with whether or not you and I . . . prosper,
as you put it. I haven't been here this month because I
couldn't get away from New York. There was a string of
conflicting commitments . . ."

"I'm sure," she said tightly, "that you've been busier
than a beaver in mud season. Nobody has to convince me
that there are people standing in line to take up your every
moment, day or night. You don't have time to come here."
Her hopeless, sweeping gesture seemed to take in the town.
"You don't have time for this. Them. Me. But why did you
start it, then?"

"Because I need this. Them. You. God!" He gave a short
laugh. "Not in that order." He sat back against the balustrade, his legs stretched before him, his expression in shadows. "Sometimes even when you're stretched to the thinnest
extension, you'll reach for something that shines out at you."

The softly spoken words disrupted the pace of her breathing all over again. Her voice, when it came, had a winded
sound, as though she had just engaged in strenuous exertion.
"Is that so?" she said. "Well, since it seems to have escaped
your notice, I'm sure you won't mind if I remind you that
we're more than pawns put on this earth to brighten Neil
Stratton's R and R from the fast lane."

A barely perceptible movement of his head brought his
face into light that caught and sparkled in the depths of his
eyes. "The Ballad of Neil and Kathy seems to be getting
tangled up with the Ballad of Neil and the Firecrackers. Do
you want me to take the blame for what happened to Eric
this afternoon? All right. If I'd been there, things probably
wouldn't have happened that way. You want to know if I
feel lousy about it? I do. And I'm going to make it up to
them. Beyond that, I don't intend to inflict the wallowings
of my guilty conscience on you. Now, about you and
me . . ."

"Thanks," she said with welling panic. "You can stop there."

"I could, but I don't want to. Kathy, I try not to be more than normally obtuse. When a lady cuts off my phone calls and returns two letters in a row, I assume she doesn't want to hear from me for a while. Tonight, I seem to be getting signals that wasn't the situation. Let's make this simple. Tell me what you want."

If there was one thing this was *not*, it was simple. Her displaced heart bucked in her throat as she thought about how ironic it was that Neil Stratton's single most disconcerting characteristic was his likelihood to ask her what she wanted. What signals? How did one disguise them? Every sane urge ordered her to tell him she never wanted to see him again. Something embedded more deeply held back the words.

In another minute he said, "So. You don't know what you want. I can understand that. Then I'll tell you—again—what I want." A smile ran like a ribbon through his words. "I want to get you into my life. You feel real to me. *I* feel real to me when I'm with you." The burning smile twisted into a mocking curve. "You don't believe me, do you? For all it penetrates, I might as well be speaking Swahili. What in the name of heaven is someone like you doing with an inferiority complex that glows like a quartz lamp? Is it something to do with having an older sister you think is better and brighter than you are? Or is this another bequest from Mr. Touchdown?"

Mr. Touchdown. He meant David. She drew back, appalled to find him so ready to do battle on this, of all numbingly hurtful issues.

"None of this has anything to do with David."

"No?" he returned quickly. "Once, when I started to love you, you cried. The second time, you froze. That had nothing to do with David?" She wasn't sure what her face showed him, but his expression softened immediately. "You misread me, darlin'. You don't have to curl away from me. You're not under attack. It came out too roughly, but I want to be sure you understand that I know."

"I don't know what you *think* you know, Neil," she said furiously, "but I . . . I—" Old and new conflicts and an aching uncertainty cut off her words. Here she was in a realm where there were no defenses and no remedies.

His gaze held her for a moment in a warm study. Then, gently, he said. "You worry too much, lady. It's going to work."

"Is it?" She dragged her gaze from his light, mesmeric eyes and stared into the high ruffled crown of starlight-sprinkled oak. She realized that her arms were crossed over her chest, her fingers clenched around her elbows. Body language: a protective gesture. So? Another signal? Eventually she would learn them all, and control them, and then she could see to it that Neil Stratton knew no more about her than she decided to tell him. But, as easily as that thought formed, it was replaced by another that wanted badly to give her hurt into his keeping, and to search out solutions from that cleverly abrasive intelligence.

She turned back to him. "I thought you told me you were going to solve all my problems," she said grimly, "and since then, you've *become* all my problems."

"But I will solve them all," he said, giving her a sexy, sweet half-smile. "I promised I would. The only thing I didn't promise was that I could do it overnight." He straightened slowly from the balustrade. "And to show you what a good sport I am, I'm going to remind you about the flowers. Remember? Too many roses?"

"Y-yes." He was making fun of her, of course, but by now she was grateful for any excuse to stay angry. "Yes! What did you mean by sending me that many flowers?"

A teasing glint in his eyes completely belied his sheepish expression. "A small token of my esteem," he said.

"And that's all you have to say about it?" Her voice was stern enough, but she could feel herself weakening.

"There's an explanation, but it's so lame that I hesitate to—" He stopped suddenly, and, bending easily from the waist, gently lifted something from a pile of leaves in the balustrade's heavy shadow. "Well," he said, smiling into the cup of his palms, "what have we here?"

Pretending not to be interested, she said, "You hesitate to what?"

"I hesitate to limp it out. And I'm not sure that you'd find the truth especially . . ." Neil's voice tapered as though the object he was examining inside his fingers distracted him so much that he forgot what he intended to say.

"Probably I wouldn't," she persevered, working to stay on course and out of this new game of his. "And I wonder if you fully appreciate what it was like for me to receive offers to pose nude for a notorious magazine."

"Oh, no," was his offhand reply, as he smiled into his fingers. "Now *that* I fully appreciate. Once, the same thing happened to me."

Words failed her—almost. "Did it?" she asked sweetly, well aware that she would no doubt regret it.

"Yes, indeed. A women's magazine asked me to do a nude centerfold. Instant internal panic. Would the relentlessly normal private endowments stand up to public expectations? So to speak—"

Hands on hips, she repeated grimly, "So to speak."

"So I did the same thing you did." His head tilted sideways to direct the smile at her. "I pretended to be indignant and turned the whole tacky deal down flat. The only sane response—a quick retreat into moral outrage."

"I'll have you know I wasn't just pretending to be indignant. I—" Finally, as his attention shifted back to his cupped hands, goaded beyond restraint, she said, "Neil, what are you doing?" He looked at her questioningly. "What's in your hand?"

"This? It's a tiny little frog. Want to see him?"

"No."

"Want to give him a kiss?" he said, offering his cupped fingers. "C'mon. One small kiss. What's the matter, don't you believe in fairy tales?" As she stood still and severe with her lips tickling dangerously at the corners as though a smile might rest close to the surface, Stratton looked back into his hands and gave an apologetic shrug. "Sorry, pal," he said. "What was that?" He held the frog to his ear, and listened for a moment. "No," he said to his hands, "this lady's a class act. She'd never go along with something like that. But you've got a lot of imagination for a frog."

The long-resisted smile finally broke onto her mouth. "Do you really have a frog there?"

"Why, sure I do." He held his hands up to his ear again. "He says if I let him go, he'll consent to allow you to kiss me instead of him." He knelt, opening his hands carefully to release his tiny captive, and stood.

She stared at him, her eyes wide, her blond hair whipping around her face in the night wind. Her small chin was tilted a bit defiantly, and he gazed steadily back at her with a fleeting smile on his lips. And then, with a movement as soft and as imperceptible as the motion of the fox that flitted across the rear of the park, they were in each other's arms, their lips meeting bruisingly in a hot, fevered exploration, her hands on his broad back, his hands flat on the taut swell of her hips, pushing him into her with a force that was ruthless in its urgency. She had no thought of resistance but allowed him to mold her to him. She felt passion rising powerfully from deep inside her, like a hidden wave in the depths of the sea rising to the surface to thrust gloriously into the moist, salty air above, meeting the granite strength of his desire.

"I want to be alone with you now, Kathy," he whispered almost fiercely. "Can we go to your apartment?"

She dragged her lips from his in a parting that was almost as sensually exciting as the meeting had been, and laid her head on his chest, and thought of her bedroom, with the photo albums, the picture of David on her nightstand, the mementoes and memories. Then she pulled back and shook her head no, her eyes wet with tears and desire. Her breasts ached for his touch.

He gently stroked her hair, a reassuring gesture, as though he knew her thoughts.

She swallowed, and said, dazed with desire and insecurity, and a feeling of tragedy, "There's—there's a motel on Highway 21 . . ."

He pulled her back to him, kissing her on the top of her head, laughing. "Oh, Kathy."

"Neil, don't laugh at me. Please."

"Never, darlin'," he said tenderly. "I'm not laughing at you. I'm laughing at us. Kathy, I didn't send you two hundred dozen roses to take you to a motel on Highway 21. This is a romance, not an affair." His fingers laid a gentle massage on the curves of her shoulders. "Kathy, I've got to leave. Because, for one thing, if I don't go now, in another five minutes I'll probably be trying to arrange you prone in the rear space of the MG Mini I'm driving. I'm going to go back to New York and try to dig some free days out of my schedule. Somehow I'll find a way for us to be together. Then I'll call you. Will you come?"

"Neil, I— No. I don't think so. Neil, I'm not sure..."

Ignoring her confused murmurs, he quieted her lips with the soft touch of his mouth. "I'll call you, Kathy," he whispered. "Sweet dreams."

7

Two NIGHTS LATER, the telephone's tinny bray woke Kathy from a sound sleep. Rueing the day Alexander Graham Bell became an inventor, Kathy peered blurrily at the glowing clock face. Two A.M. As far as she knew, there were only two categories of folk who called at that hour—drunks with the wrong number, and twelve-year-old boys with extensions in their bedrooms.

She rolled over, groaning and pulling the pillow over her head. Twelve shrill rings crept through her pillow and into her unreceptive eardrums before she stuck out a hand, groped blindly, found the receiver, and dragged it underneath the pillow with her.

"Mmmmmf?" she said.

She was answered immediately by the martial tones of a bugle playing reveille. Four bars into the melody, the tune stopped on one note and repeated it over and over until it was interrupted by the unpleasant screech of a needle being forced off a skipping record. And then a slightly husky male radio announcer voice said, "Congratulations! This is radio station WILT-FM 98.6 your radio dial, and your name has been selected at random from over seven hundred million entrants nationwide to participate in our Trip to Venus Sweepstakes. Ms. Carter, if you can identify the following song, you'll be the winner of an all-expense-paid trip to Venus, or any other planet of your choice, moons of Neptune excluded." There was a series of electronic blips as someone picked out a tune on a touch-tone phone panel.

Had the voice been disguised twice as well, she would have recognized the sense of humor. For two days of fretting and indecision, she had waited for him to call. New life began to thump through her sleepy heart.

The blipped-out version of "Oh Susannah" came to an end, and the voice asked her politely for her answer.

"The Volga Boatman," she said groggily.

"I'm sorry, that's not correct. But we have a very special consolation prize for you this morning. You will be flown free of charge from the nearest commercial airport coach class, for three days with rock legend Neil Stratton. You will breakfast on fruit yogurt and white bread served by the singer himself—"

"Stratton . . ." she began.

"And experience nights of unparalleled and exquisite passion, filled with fanciful, sensual delight, shared with the famous idol on his hand-monogrammed satin sheets."

She pulled the receiver from her ear, looked at it owlishy, and then said in sleep-slurred tones, "Neil, it's two o'clock in the morning."

"That's no trouble for us, ma'am. We're an all night radio station. When would you like to schedule your trip?"

"July 30th, in the year 2072," she muttered.

"All coach class flights are booked on that day. Can you give us another option? We're flexible."

Kathy felt her heart shift into overdrive. "Well, I'm not." Rubbing her itchy nose with the back of her hand, she said, "Look, I'm sorry but it's impossible. I can't come."

Pause. Then the voice said hopefully, "Got any friends?"

Choked laughter stirred in her throat. "Neil, have you been drinking?"

"I have to admit to hittin' Jack Daniels."

"Do you mean," she said, "that you've had the nerve to call me at this hour of the morning after a drunken brawl? And who's Jack Daniels?"

"He's a whiskey, my innocent. What are you doing at this hour?"

"Trying to sleep," she said pointedly.

"No, no, I mean right now."

Vaguely confused by his quick shifts, she said, "Well— now? Lying in bed listening to you on the phone."

"What are you wearing?" After a moment of unforth-coming silence from her, he said coaxingly, "Be nice to me. Feed my fantasies. What've you got on?"

She readjusted a twisted fold in the top of her short cotton nightgown. Suppressing a laugh, she murmured, "A rubber raincoat. How's that?"

"It has promise. Personally, I could see you in transparent vinyl, red cowboy boots, and nothing else." There was another pause. When he spoke again, the playfulness was gone and his voice was soft. "Come to me, Kathy."

She sat up dazedly and ran a long, graceful hand through her dark hair, raking it from her face. "Neil . . ."

"Please."

How rich-toned, how sincere his voice could become. She said glumly, "Said the spider to the fly."

"Kathy—" Only one word, yet he managed to invest in it so much sensual promise, such beguiling tenderness, that the breath caught like warm liquid in her lungs. Very gently he said, "Aren't you getting weary of fighting this, darlin'?"

Hot and cold currents were flooding with such quick changes in her body that she felt pummeled to the soul. "I can't do it, Neil, I just can't. There's the shop."

"Renee will watch it."

"I can't just ask Renee to watch the shop for me, not for more than a few hours."

"You won't have to ask her. I already did."

"Neil, if you called my sister at two o'clock in the morning . . ."

"No, I talked to her last night."

"And why did you call her in the evening and me at this hour?"

"I couldn't get back to a phone. I've been working. Working, drinking, thinking about you, eating the most god-awful take-out Chinese food, and breathing stale cigarette smoke. I miss you. I need you. But I want you to come to me because you're ready, not because I've pushed you into it, so I'm only going to ask you once more. Will you come and see me, lady?"

There it was, dealt with the same easy charm as his gently teasing lead-ins, but she had discovered, by now, how to tell when he was no longer teasing. This was an ultimatum, a test, and, for her, a possible way out. Beneath the playfulness and the courtesy, Stratton was asking her to come or to have a very good reason why she could not, and if she did neither thing, he would not continue to press her. Nor would he chain himself in a commitment that left his needs unmet. He might continue to ask her to be with him, but he was hardly likely to go hungry in the meantime.

Though he had never said as much to her, in his work there was more than Jack Daniels and stale cigarette smoke. There were pressures and temptations around him that had crushed many other men and women in his position. Guesses, intuition, and imagination together were probably not enough to help her understand what it must be like on the top rung of his fast-paced world. Not once had he held it over her head; but there was no need for Neil Stratton to be lonely, or to plead for a woman's company, or even, perhaps, to court and pursue a reluctant companion as he had done with her. I'm only going to ask you once more, lady, he had said—and he didn't call *that* pushing her?

Finally, overcome by a feeling of being backed into a corner, she snapped back at him like a frightened puppy. "The reason you go through women so fast is not that you're so promiscuous, Stratton. You just drive them crazy. That's why you have to work that hard. You have to support them all in the rest home where you have them stashed away. How can I come to see you? I don't even know where you are."

"I'm in New York right now, but tomorrow I'll be in Tennessee," he said, receiving her outburst calmly.

"Of course you wouldn't be any longer than one day in any one place. So you'll be in Tennessee. Fine. I'll fly down in my Lear jet," she said.

"Better yet, fly down in *my* Lear jet."

"Sure, Neil, coach class on your Lear. Do I get to the airport in a chauffeured limousine?"

"It'll be at your door tomorrow morning at eight."

"I believe you. He's going to drive out from New York and be here in six hours. Guess he's a fast driver, like at the Indian—" Kathy yawned. "Indianapolis 500 . . ." There was a cool, comfortable breeze coming in the window, and she snuggled into her bed, drawing her knees up, cradling the receiver against her hair, and rather helplessly giving herself over to the low, honeyed tone of his voice.

"Do you want something more exotic? How about a magic carpet?" he said. "Nothing's impossible for someone who feels the way I do about you . . ."

Distant sound penetrated her sleep. Kathy lay wrapped in her cool sheets, daylight tickling her lashes. A faint, high-pitched electric hum was coming from somewhere close by. She opened one eye, and saw that the noise came from a giant fuzzy-looking telephone receiver, magnified by proximity. A hand came out of nowhere and lifted it away, and Kathy heard the plastic clack as it was hung up.

"Good morning!" came Renee's cheery voice. "Sit up, Kath. I'll be back in a minute." Mystified, Kathy did as she was told, and Renee reappeared from the kitchen bearing a plastic lap tray set with a plate of quiche, orange juice, and a steaming teapot.

"My birthday," Kathy said blankly.

Renee caught a piece of the quiche on a fork, which she then placed in Kathy's hand, curling Kathy's lax fingers firmly around it. "No, guess again."

"Mmmm, this is wonderful. Heavenly," Kathy said with her mouth full. "Is this green tea? Yum." She sipped from the cup, then directed an uneasy glance at the phone on her bedstand. "Was the telephone in bed with me this morning?"

"Yes. Ve zy-cologists haf a name for zis." The accent was Austrian. "Ve call zi sickness phonophilia—ze unnatural erotic attachment to telephones. Odd that Doktor Freud failed to mention it in his writings. By ze vay," she added, "did you haf any strange dreams last night?"

"Very strange. As a matter of—" She stopped suddenly as the floating memories coalesced. "All right. What's going on?"

"Keep eating," Renee ordered. "It's seven-thirty, sluga-bed. In two hours—" she picked up a silver teaspoon which had been Aunt Betty's—"this will be you." Her fingers walked across the tray to the spoon and hopped inside, and then lifted it into the air, making a noise with her mouth like air escaping a balloon. "Rocketing through the air for a hideaway rendezvous with the man of your dreams." She landed the spoon and then made the fingers of her other hand walk up to it, and the four fingers became entangled in a passionate embrace.

With the quiche turning to a lump in her stomach, Kathy put her teacup down and flopped a distracted hand on the top of her hair in a shaken gesture. "Then it *is* true. You mean you actually encouraged him to believe that I— I can't even remember what happened. I was talking to him on the telephone . . . and then I guess I went to sleep."

"He said it was very touching. You were snoring into the mouthpiece."

"You talked to him this morning?" Kathy asked unsteadily.

"Bright and early. There's a car coming for you in half an hour."

"Madness!" said Kathy, and flopped back down on the bed.

"Nonsense," said Renee bracingly. "It'll do wonders for you to get away for a few days."

"It won't be getting away. It'll be going *to*."

"Hurry up; your bath water's getting cold."

"Bath water!" groaned Kathy. "Yeeks! I feel like a mail-order bride."

"I can see you're too excited to eat," said Renee, removing the tray from Kathy's lap. "Let's go—into the tub."

Kathy wandered unwillingly into the bathroom and pulled off her nightgown, but sat on the edge of the tub, trailing her fingers in the water.

"Bathe!" called her sister from outside the door.

"Bathe; perfume your body with scented oils; prepare yourself for the Caliph," Kathy called back crossly. "Is this homework for a correspondence course on becoming a madam? I don't trust you anyway. You're in league with Neil. As far as you're concerned, that man's the bee's knees."

"The bee's knees I don't know, but no red-blooded

woman can look at that man without wanting his honey. Do you want your curling iron?"

"No." Kathy lifted herself carefully over the high sides of the lion's-paws bathtub and into the stingingly warm water. "Are you packing for me? It'll be wasted. I'm not going."

"Yeah, yeah. Kath, I've stuck in some of the play clothes I picked up in that nifty little boutique in Honolulu this spring. What're you wearing on the plane? How about that copper-colored dress? Y'know, the Egyptian cotton with the bib top?"

Emerging from the washcloth with a face dappled in bubbles, Kathy said, "I don't know what made me buy that thing. It clings and since it hasn't got a back, there's no way to wear a bra with the darn thing."

"Sveet-heart," came the Austrian accent, "you haf to give ze man ze message that you're a voman."

"Can't I send him a registered letter instead?" Kathy asked, sinking into the tub. "Anyway, I don't think he needs reminding. And I'm *not going*."

She was still saying that to herself one hour and fifteen minutes after the Lear jet had left Madison's truax field, as it landed in Tennessee at a remote airstrip owned by a timber company. Kathy's anxious glances out the window had revealed green rolling hills hung with mist around inlaid lakes that shone like lapis jewels. She stepped out onto hot asphalt and the minty sting of pine. Highland crickets piped from the golden grass that edged the cleared ground around the airstrip. Beyond was a jutting sea of evergreen forest, and Kathy followed their jagged skyline until her gaze dropped to a knot of cars. There, as though he had summoned her attention by some subliminal signal, Kathy saw Neil.

He must have seen her first, because the uninhibited sweep of his arm threw her a kiss as he walked toward her. A lump formed in her throat and she could not seem to stop the way her body registered his increasing nearness like the jumping needle on an earthquake register. The long drape of thigh and calf strained against low-slung jeans belted in heavy rawhide. He was close enough now for her to make out that the white silkscreen print on his navy t-shirt was the Mad Hatter's Tea Party illustration from *Alice in Won-*

derland. Before she could see it, she felt the spirit of a grin that teased his lips, and the rich, welcoming glow in his eyes.

It might have made a more poetic picture if she had run into his arms, but Kathy hung back in the sharp shadow of the jet, caught in a wave of irrational shyness. She was conscious that her head was held chin-high, that her hands rested with open fingers in the copper folds of her skirt, that her knees were steady. The "I'm not coming" had begun to regroup into an "I'm not here. I'm not here."

Very aware of the pilot and co-pilot beside her, she hoped that Neil would not meet her with an embrace, though it hardly surprised her that she felt deflated when he did not. Smiling warmly, he said hello to her and the pilots, greeting them by name, asking questions about the flight, and thanking them.

The amenities completed, she walked alone with Neil toward the cars, their feet disappearing into the tall, limp grass, her skirt swaying within inches of his jeans. On his other side, he carried her suitcase, but his free hand and hers might have touched at the lightest movement. Reality was swiftly intruding on the play world of denial. It was no small decision she had made, that required this thick a cerebral cushion. Peripheral vision revealed that he was studying her face.

Grabbing at words, she said, "I didn't know a jet could land at an airstrip this small."

"Oh, yes," he said. "All a jet needs is four thousand plus feet of good runway and some government-certified soul on the ground to radio up weather information. There's no way around it, pretty lady. You're here."

His sharp intuition made her gasp. His hand lifted and the back of his fingers affectionately stroked the flesh of her bare shoulder. "I wasn't sure you'd come. Your sister told me you'd never been away from home before."

There was no condescension in his tone; that hardly made the statement less irritating.

"David and I used to drive to Chicago all the time for baseball games," she retorted too quickly, "and sometimes we stayed overnight at a Holiday Inn." Feeble, Kathy. Really feeble. Shape up, calm down, and stop trying so hard. She smiled lopsidedly at the spearing pines. "That was pretty preposterous, wasn't it? Obviously I can't out-sophisticate you."

"Were we having a sophistication contest? Damn! And me without my French phrasebook and beret. *Eh bien, cherie.* How is our *petit fils* Eric?"

"Eric? He's been following your advice to the letter."

"How alarming," he said. "Which advice is that?"

"To listen to the doctors so he'll be able to play in time for the county fair. Please don't do anything more with the French accent. I've already had an Austrian psychologist before breakfast."

"Sorry." He was smiling. "You expect me to be sophisticated, and I didn't want to disappoint you. How are Mike and Sticks taking things?"

"Much better since the time you spent with them yesterday on the phone. You still speak their language. Can I borrow your teenage phrase book?"

"You don't need it. What you've got works much better."

She turned to him, beginning to bristle. "And what, pray, have I got?"

He had turned also, his eyes glowing like faceted turquoise gems. "Character."

Three cars edged the strip: an old station wagon; a hulking, rusted four-door checker cab with an "I Brake for Animals" bumper sticker; and a highly waxed Maserati convertible.

Kathy put her hand on the latch of the Maserati and started to pull it open, but paused in surprise as Neil opened the trunk of the big old four-door and laid her luggage in it. When he closed it again, it clanged like a bank vault.

"They don't make 'em like they used to. Solid metal," he said.

He was eyeing the gargantuan heap with such affectionate warmth that Kathy suddenly realized she was standing by the wrong car. *That* was Neil's real car? He held open a rust-bitten door for her, and she walked around the Maserati and over to the Checker. The interior was roomy and clean, if a little worn, and there was a bundle of letters on the seat beside her.

"Hold the glove compartment closed there, darlin', while I shut the door," he cautioned.

"Why? Will it dump ice in my lap?"

"No," he said, and slammed the door. He looked in at her, smiling. "Greasy wrenches." Sliding in beside her, he leaned past her and covered the glove compartment with his own hand as he shut his own door. He turned the ignition. The engine throbbed like a tank's. "She's a 1952 Checker cab. She'll run through a tornado. I bought her for three hundred dollars my second year in college. What's the matter?"

"It's a rust bucket, Stratton."

He coasted over the grass to a blacktop road lined with pine trees. "I'll be the first to admit that she could use a little body work, but I'm kind of set on letting her age naturally. I'll love you, too, when you get old and rusty. Put on your seatbelt. Not that one. Come next to me."

Something held her back. She stayed where she was and firmly latched herself in. "No, thanks; I like to sit by the window. And I don't want to crush your mail." The mail. A safe subject.

"That?" he said, glancing at the bundle. "Chuck it in back."

"Aren't you going to look at it? That's a pretty cavalier attitude to have toward mail. Out in the sticks, where I come from, we love our mail." At least her voice was beginning to sound normal.

"I have a filing system," he said. "I toss it piece by piece over my shoulder. Envelopes that land on the floor left of the hump, I throw out; the right side means maybe later."

"Fan letters included?"

"Those come to my office in Los Angeles. They handle most of it—requests for sheets I've slept on, my hand in marriage . . . And then there are the long letters telling me how wonderful I am." He grinned. "Those they forward. The little stack here usually goes to my secretary, but she's taking a few vacation days."

"Let's see how the system works." The seat behind her sloped backward at a thirty-degree angle as the cab chugged up a mountain grade between rough-hewn sandstone bluffs. A sign at the roadside read WATCH FOR FALLEN ROCK. She picked up the bundle and peeled back the red rubber band. "Lobe, Globe and Loebb," she read.

"Those are my lawyers. Whatever they write to me, they send in duplicate to my manager. Left side."

"Aronowitz, Inc."

"That's my manager, Mickey Aronowitz. Whatever he sends me, he sends in duplicate to my lawyers."

"Left side?" she queried.

"Left side with a vengeance."

There were four in a row then, from charitable organizations he regularly contributed to. They went into the maybe file, right of the hump: one from a famous symphony orchestra, two from foundations researching different hereditary illnesses, one from an organization fighting to preserve marine life.

The road lurched over a shallow rise and began to sink rapidly, swooping in a free fall down the undivided blacktop. Kathy felt a tug in the pit of her stomach—a feeling close to erotic. Rounded peaks spread out beyond the valley they skirted, emerald green in the sun, fading to purple, with white fog snaking between them.

"This next one is from—" It took a moment to decipher the handwriting. "Jake Overton."

"Start a new pile on the back seat," he said. "We'll call it From Old Friends Wanting to Borrow Money. Forward to Accountant."

There were five more in the reject pile, and the last was a dainty lavender envelope. "This one has no return address. Just a pansy in the upper left-hand corner."

"That's from Sandy," he said, with a little smile. "You could open it."

Sandy. It was the only letter he was interested in. The name struck a faint chord. A turkey sandwich on wheat bread rose in her mind. "Sandy," she mused. "The one who packs you too much lunch?"

"You have a good memory," he said. The old car swayed as it turned off the blacktop and slowed to forty miles an hour on a road of red dirt. A vermilion dust followed behind, feathering in light-spangled flecks into the tall pines on either side. Inside the envelope, Kathy found a lavender note card, embossed with the pansy emblem again, and a heady perfume filled the car as she unfolded the page. He must have noticed her expression, for he said, "If you've been curious as to what natural musk smells like, that's it. An acquired taste."

She wished desperately for the strength of mind to resist

wondering if he'd acquired it himself. The letter began without preamble. *"I may see you before you get this letter,"* she read aloud, *"because we're coming to New York on Sunday. Rumor has it that you're going to try and spend a day or two in Tennessee, in which case, if I know you, this letter will be tossed on the floor of that heap of yours. Bob says why write—you never answer your mail anyway. Tokyo was fantastic, except that Bob caught the flu and blamed it on having tea with no shoes on for three days. We bought you a silk kimono, thigh-length; very sexy. Everyone who talked to you in L.A. says you're working too hard—seventeen hours a day and no partying—and that you're more serious than ever about that scene you've got going in Wisconsin . . ."*

Surprised and intimidated by the idea of distant speculation about her, Kathy's voice trailed off. In the ensuing pause, Neil said helpfully, "She's referring to you."

Kathy found her voice. "I guessed." She blinked and cleared her throat and read on:

"Be warned: Mickey A. is arriving fresh from Nice and he told Bob on the phone Tuesday that he was going to 'try and talk some sense into you,' whatever that means. Nothing much happening in L.A., except the bash for Bruce, who's in town this week. There were a lot of TV people there; expensive booze. Bruce stayed for ten minutes; he was smart. Hangover city. Be glad you missed it. No more news, except that I stopped by your office last night and picked up a piece of fan mail I thought you'd like to see. It had hand-crocheted bikini underwear for you and started out 'Neil, darling, I'm writing this while lying naked in a hammock.' It was a real doozy. But the boys were over last night and got into it—there was much ho-hoing and someone made off with bikini and letter. Your girl in Hollywood, San. P.S. Bob wants to know when you're going to introduce Miss Wisconsin to us. Whatsamatter, are you afraid of scaring her off?"

Stuffing the note back with difficulty into an envelope that seemed to have shrunk, Kathy stared out at the fragrant vista of passing evergreens. "It must be nice," she said slowly, "to have so many people interested in your welfare. What's it like to be loved by the world?"

"The world," he said, watching the road, "is a very kinky

lover. It's likely to want too much of certain parts of you, and nothing at all of others."

The calm, almost prosaic irony of his tone belied the world-weariness of his words. Fighting to understand him better, Kathy asked, "Are you tired of it, Neil? Does a person get too much glamour?"

"A person gets too much *false* glamour." A leisurely twist of his hand headed the cab from the red dirt road to a primitive, rutted track. "We're coming to the beginning of my land."

There was a hand-lettered sign: NO HUNTING. She thought of David, and his blaze orange jacket. It suddenly occurred to her that she had no idea where Neil was taking her. All she knew was that he had some kind of a "place." It could be an antebellum mansion with tall white columns or a futuristically designed fashionable A-frame. Thinking of the car, she looked forward to finding out with a mixture of amusement and dread. What lay at the end of this bumpy, sun-washed lane? The area was heavily forested, with thick underbrush. She could have sworn she saw a deer leaping away from them into the shadowed woods as the car passed. Patches of pink and purple asters and bright-eyed field daisies flourished among the tall grasses and wild millet growing by the roadside. "How much land do you own here?" she asked.

"A little more than eight hundred acres, not including the lake. Do you like to swim?"

"Oh, yes. Sure. Neil, I assume . . . you—you have some sort of a dwelling here, don't you?" The car hit a bump and Neil reached quickly in front of her to hold the glove compartment door.

"Yes. A little place," he said.

"Do you have other company, or—" Oh, God, why did it have to come out so clumsily? She plunged on. "Or are we going to be alone?"

His answer was soft and textured, comfortable, like the warm wind that touched her face, like the fluting call of the mockingbird that came from the forest. "We're going to be alone." He gave her a swift sideways glance. "Do you mind?"

It was too late to mind and too soon to know whether or not she should mind. The smile she gave back to him was weak and seemed awkwardly influenced by the high-pressure pump of her heart. "I don't think I'd be here if I minded."

Her voice had a wavering conviction that he must have heard, for she saw his mouth tilt up at the corner. The vegetation fell abruptly away as the big old car lumbered into a clearing and rolled to a stop as Stratton's hand moved to the key. His wrist turned and the great engine wound down with the roar of a World War I biplane in a crash dive.

Before her, dwarfed by majestic pine trees, slumbering beneath sunbeams dancing with dust motes, a small and beautiful log cabin rested on a slight hillock. A burst of blue-lace flowers rippled at the base of the little rise. The cabin was of saddle-notch construction, the logs gray-patinaed by weathering, and bees hummed, tiny yellow darts near the chimney of creek stones chinked with red clay and slaked lime. The scene, filled with homey dignity, stood like a monument to early America.

8

KATHY JUMPED OUT of the car, scarcely realizing that the door handle came off in her hand as she closed the door. The mossy ground gave like a carpet beneath her feet as she walked toward the cabin, falling in love all over again with Colonial America. "Neil, what a wonderful house! What did you do, evict Abe Lincoln?"

"In these parts, it would have been Davy Crockett," he said, politely removing the door handle from her hand and tossing it onto the front seat of the car.

"Davy Crockett? Really?"

"No. Not really. As far as I know, he never came near the place," Neil said, his voice muffled as he put his head into the trunk to get her luggage. "This land was owned by six generations of a family that ran a sawmill nearby. This place had been abandoned for thirty years before I bought the land, but they left a nice feeling behind. Go ahead in; the door's open."

She stepped inside. A large fireplace with its soft ochre stonework dominated a beam-ceilinged room laid with bright rag rugs and a cherry table of country Hepplewhite. Open pine shelves drooped their scalloped edges along a

wall and Kathy smiled over the canisters of whole wheat
flour and hominy grits, copper cooking vessels, intriguingly
covered baskets and colorful kitchenware. Beneath was a
very old oak icebox with a glass-paneled candle lantern on
it. On the opposite wall, an Audubon print of a meadow
mouse adorned the space between chintz-hung windows.

"And you call me an old-fashioned girl," she said finally.
"There's no electricity?"

"Not a watt," he said.

"And the hot and cold running water . . . ?"

He went to the copper sink and pulled on the handle of
the pump three times—squeak, squeak, squeak—and a
clear stream splashed out. He smiled and shrugged. "And
I'll bet you thought I was a pampered pop hero who couldn't
do anything for himself."

She hadn't expected any of it—the beautiful little cabin,
the old clunker of a car that he loved. It touched her. And
his smile touched her also, half-derisive, more magical than
vulnerable, the smile of a person in contact with his own
failings and strengths, reaching out to her like a warm hand-
clasp. Across the room, she could feel the unspoken communication. He couldn't have known it was her lifelong
desire to spend a night in a log cabin, yet here it was, in
an almost eerie dream-wish fulfillment. Every year she had
blown out the ever increasing set of candles to that wish,
never telling. It had worked!

Under a spell of heavenly charm, she wandered through
an open doorway into the second room where steeply pitched
roof beams hung over a rope bed of curly maple laid with
a bright quilt in a rising star pattern that reminded her of
her own quilt at home.

Her eyes strayed to the graceful form of Neil's old guitar,
leaning against a beautiful Shaker cupboard. She studied
the guitar. Yes. It was the one she had fixed for him last
spring. Her mind filled with the memory of awakening on
her back-room couch, of his first lightly searching kiss.
Before her heating blood had begun gathering in her cheeks,
she found herself looking back toward the pretty, waiting
bed.

The cabin floor was not the sort anyone could sneak
across. The floorboards crooned under Neil's light footfalls

as he came to her and carefully put his hand under her chin to lift her face.

"There are times," he said gently, "when you are too transparent, Kathy Carter." He bent slightly to bring his mouth into delicate contact with hers, his thumb in a slow, rotating caress that paused at the corner of her lip. Then his hand moved, drawing back her hair to uncover the back of her neck, and he touched her there with his mouth, light, glancing kisses up to her hairline.

"Poor Kathy," he said. "So many hurdles..." She felt his lips tighten against her as he smiled. "Don't worry about the bed. I'll work out a couple of scripts and you can choose the one you like best. For example: we could pretend we each think the other one is going to sleep in the car. After we blow out the candles, you slip into the right side of the bed, I'll slip into the left, and then we'll act real surprised to see each other. What it lacks in the romance department, it would make up in comic relief. We could work in the romance later."

She wanted badly to turn to him and say, "Don't tease me, Neil. I think I love you. I wouldn't have come here if I didn't." Her feelings for him had become a trap with the jaws closed. The more she tried to pull away, the more she was hurt. So she stayed quiet and vulnerable, trying to trust her feelings, hoping that with time he would free the trap and heal her. She looked at him, her lips closed and her expression grave. Her blond hair fell in a wave over one eye. Smiling into her eyes, he tucked it behind her ear and moved his head to nuzzle her earlobe with his lips.

"Smile for me," he said, and when she did, tensely, he touched her cheek and, walking past her, set her suitcase on the bed. "Why don't you change? We'll go to the lake and fish for dinner. I'll meet you in the barn out back." He smiled at her again and was gone.

She stood in the center of the room for half a minute, and then opened the suitcase. Renee's clothes, all of them, she realized with rueful surprise. Very expensive material, extremely revealing. She picked up a string bikini—enough fabric there to fill a mouse hole. Kathy tried on a few of the t-shirts. Her bra straps showed beneath them all, so she shed herself of that garment, before settling on a brief strawberry-colored camisole and matching shorts. Slipping into suede sandals with walking soles, she took a deep breath to calm herself, paused on the way out to touch the mantel and run her hand down the rough wood door frame, and then stepped out into the dry, piney air.

The "barn out back" proved to be a low shed of much later construction. Neil stood with his back to her expertly splitting firewood with a kindling axe. A block of wood fell to the ground in a chunky clatter, and he saw her as he turned to get another.

"Are we really going to fish for dinner?" she asked brightly, trying to appear normal in what seemed to her a state of nakedness. "I thought we'd go out and skin us up a coon."

Neil had set down the hatchet behind him, his eyes never leaving her. "I'm thinking," he said, his gaze making an unhurried journey from the dainty tips of her toes to her shining blond hair, "of changing the menu altogether."

His gaze, lingering casually on the strip of ivory skin above her shorts where she had tried unsuccessfully to pull the waistband high enough to cover her navel, was leaving her with no doubt about his revised plans. Insecurity mixed with another, more earthy emotion as she fought the urge to retreat, to cover her exposed midriff with her hands. Kath, try not to act like any more of a dip than you have to.

"I thought you were going to show me the lake," she managed.

"The lake," he said, with a playful half-smile, "hasn't been waiting as long as I have. Come inside with me; I'll show you what I've been wanting to do for months to those pretty toes of yours. Toes, working upward."

Desire spread with downy softness through her body— toes first, working upward. There was something in her that was becoming more accustomed to his open telegraphing of desire—something that had been missing in her relationship with David. David had been too kind to pursue her, even though he had loved and wanted her. And so neither of them had discovered until they were married that it was not her virtue but her inability to respond to him physically that had kept her so "pure." The love, forged like iron through the drifting years of friendship, had been a sister's

love for a brother masquerading as something more ele-
mental, masked always by her own unexamined high standards. And now David was gone and she was here with
Neil, alive and guilty.

His expression changed as he sensed her haunted with-
drawal and she waited with tight-throated apprehension to
see if her fence-sitting would anger him. But the moment
passed, or he forced it to pass, by catching her hand in his
and saying, "I've angled enough. Let's go fishing."

From a cedar stump, he picked up a picnic basket and
tackle pack as he led her to a sun-dappled path where pine
needles lay in a snapping carpet. Around and above them
were the pines, rugged and sapful, giving off pungent per-
fumes.

Neil's fingers, wrapped firmly around Kathy's, were
perhaps meant as a platonic comfort. For her, they had all
the comfort of sticking a hand into a light socket. They had
gone quite far before she was able to stop wishing desperately that he would turn around and take her to his beautiful
cabin and hold her, hold her until she could no longer retreat.
Her senses sought out individually the feel of each of his
strong musician's fingers at their contact point with her
hand. His touch began to intensify her perceptions until she
could feel the summer day even as she felt his warming
flesh. The path wended downhill, through a narrow valley
and over an abandoned logging railroad. Glades of honey
locust, wild roses, and blackberry lilies grew up around her.
There was another short rise and over that she could look
down a sloping plane of tall second-growth hardwoods to
the blue lake, glinting like an inverse sky.

Together, walking very close, they strolled the ribbon
of beach with the water grasses tickling her lower legs. Neil
stopped her before a wide shelf of limestone where crys-
talline fresh spring water bubbled from a natural cauldron
that spilled into the lake through a mat of ferns. While a
bottle of home-brewed apple beer from the picnic basket
chilled in the spring, they climbed on the outcropping, finding fossils and learnedly identifying them with long, preposterous Latin names, laughing freely and trying to outdo
each other in syllables and fake academic excitement.

Cross-legged on the sunny rock, they drank apple beer
and ate corn cakes, oranges, and berries from a nearby bush.

Kathy laughed as a chipmunk invited himself, and watched Neil, resting at ease on his elbow, as he fed crumbs to the furry little creature.

Afterwards, he dragged his fiberglass canoe from its shelter in a stand of tupelos and paddled her along the shoreline, showing her the track-covered areas on the beach where he had seen deer, mink, and, once, a bobcat come to drink at night. They watched a heron stepping stiffly through the feather grass as Neil baited their bamboo fishing poles. Looking quizzically at the prow, he said, "Look behind you, on the deck. I think that's a mouse nest."

Just as she looked, a tiny field mouse poked its nose out of a small mound of grass and twigs and fixed them with a stern eye before disappearing. They both laughed.

"A stowaway," she said.

"Shall we serenade him? Sing with me. What do you like besides *Camelot?*"

Later, she wasn't sure how he'd been able to coax her into blending her true-toned but underbodied soprano with his lush, huskily sensual voice, but they had harmonized on an old Dylan song and a couple of very old Hank Williams melodies before she became embarrassed enough by her own inadequacy to say firmly, "No more. We'll scare the fish."

Neil apparently either didn't notice any inadequacy, or was too nice to say so. "On the contrary, I'm using your voice as a lure. Have you ever thought of singing professionally?"

His words couldn't be anything more than a tease and she was thinking of tossing a playful sprinkle of lake water on him when the tip of her pole jerked violently.

"There!" he said. "You see, it works! You've got a bite."

"It must be Charlie the tuna," she said. "The fish with bad taste. What do I do now?"

"Haul him in. Want help?"

"No way. Keep your mitts off Charlie," she said, dragging at the pole, which seemed suddenly to weigh a ton. The canoe took a radical dip as she shifted on her seat.

"Kathy, be careful—" Neil said. She braced her feet and tried to jerk the pole back and, in a flashing swirl of plummeting gravity, the canoe slid out from underneath them and threw them into the water.

Fighting the sudden cool water, her hair and clothes soaking and water rushing unpleasantly into the open channels of her nose and ears, she felt Neil's hands take a tight grip on her shoulders.

"Stand up, Kathy!" he said. "Honey, put your feet down! God, I've never seen anyone try so hard to drown in four feet of water."

She found her feet and saw Neil standing in front of her, coughing and pushing wet hair away from his eyes. They were soaked through, water streaming down their faces, the water up to her shoulders and his chest. Her bamboo fishing rod floated by to her right and with a quick lunge, she caught it up and gathered in the line. The end was empty. Fish and bait had vanished. She frowned furiously at the bare hook and heard Neil's gasping laughter.

"It looks like—Charlie's made a clean break for it," he panted.

"Listen to you wheeze," she said, facing him indignantly. "And after shouting at *me* about trying to drown! You look like you've—" laughter began to choke up in her throat— "you've swallowed half the—" helpless laughter until she could manage to spit out the word, "lake. Y'know what? I think Charlie rammed us. No. Quit laughing! I mean it. We were rammed! He was big as a—" scrambling for comparisons—"big as a skateboard." Her hands spread out to show him the size of a big fish.

"He was as big as a go-cart." He used his hands to show her a bigger fish.

She flung her hands out at her sides. "He was big as a Volkswagen!"

"It was the Loch Ness monster!"

Their arms were wide, and they were standing close. Their t-shirts were wet and form-fitting, hiding nothing. And it was he who pulled her to him, into his arms. She was light in the water as he cupped her hips to him and they were still laughing as he brought his lips down on hers. Her wet hair flowed around them like an aura, and his kiss tasted incredibly sweet to her. She could break away from it only long enough to cover his cheek with hungry little skimming kisses, drinking the water from his flesh, returning again to his mouth.

She drew back suddenly, starting to laugh again, pointing

toward the canoe. "Neil, look! The mouse!"

The field mouse was huddled on the edge of the half-submerged canoe, shivering in its wet coat and eyeing them with nose-twitching disfavor as they broke off their embrace and pulled the canoe toward shore. It leapt off and swam the last few feet to the bank, shook itself dry on a round rock, and gave them one last disgusted glance before scampering into the grass.

"That's the last time he'll ever let us take him for a ride," Neil said.

Happy and wet, warm in the sunlight, they pulled the canoe from the water, tipping it upside down. Neil walked back in the lake to snag the paddles where they had washed close to shore about twenty yards away. All around was an open, sloping meadow, forest-edged, of clover blooming in red and pink. While Neil was retrieving the paddles, Kathy walked up the hillside and, finding a place where the clover was good and deep, kicked off her limp sandals and threw herself on her back. The sun was high in a cloudless heaven. She heard bees hum and the twittering of birds, and a low song of the dogwood maples, white oak and hickory moving in the affectionate combing of the summer breeze.

Neil tossed the paddles next to the canoe and came to lie beside her on his back, chewing a long stem of grass. Neither of them spoke for five minutes. Finally he sat up, pulled off his t-shirt, and wrung it out, before tossing it aside and lying back down, propping himself up on one elbow, and looking her over.

The clover was tall in late summer, and very still around them. All they could see was sky and clover. They were together in a nest, a hidden place. She looked back at him steadily, her chin tilted almost fearlessly as, with an enigmatic and quietly humorous half-smile, he let his gaze wander over her, lingering for arousing moments where her water-taunted nipples strained darkly against the dampened cloth, then over the curve of her hips and carefully down her bare legs.

"You win the wet t-shirt contest," he said.

Apple beer, sunshine, and laughter were a powerful combination, and Kathy, feeling free, glowing, and a little silly, propped herself up on her elbows, her mouth open in mock surprise. "Oh, yeah? What do I win?" she said.

He lazily lifted his index finger and hooked it into the neckline of her t-shirt, following the line of the yoke first up one side to her shoulder, then across her collarbone to the other side. The wet cloth parted from its clinging to her skin and then, pressing back down, made an interesting tickling sensation wherever his fingertip did its work. His finger traced all the way to her shoulder and gently pulled the cloth in a smooth movement until her creamy skin came into view.

"I'm thinking it over," he said. "Any suggestions?"

"I hesitate to offer any," she replied. "Last time I won a contest I ended up in a Lear jet."

His fingers were lightly touching across her neck and came to rest on her ear. "Maybe I can take you back up to forty thousand feet."

"Promises, promises."

He chuckled huskily, and his hooked finger pulled some more, the fabric coming halfway down her upper arm, baring the dampened, rounded skin of her breast, ivory in shade, delicately traced with the lightest of blue veins, and showing, where skin and fabric met, a slim crescent of pink. Her chest began a slow, visible rise and fall as his eyes lingered there. "Miss Jones," he murmured, "hold all my calls." And then, carefully, deliberately, he brought his lips down on hers, so slowly that she felt them coming before they touched her own, a kiss that began before it had begun. Just before she could no longer support herself up on her elbows, his broad hand on her back laid her down, his mouth not breaking contact with hers. He entangled her fingers in his and drifted their locked hands down until her arm was straight, then pulled her t-shirt the rest of the way until the fragile skin of her shoulders and breasts were free to the summer's kiss, and to his own.

Melting inside, like a candy with a liquid center, her heart was throbbingly aware of his hand touching warmth to the surface of her flesh, and then he covered her with the textured heat of his chest, pressing her into him. She felt enveloped by softness and natural care, the clover and his arms at her back, the light, warm breath of the breeze and his body covering her. He held her slightly elevated, and as her head dropped back, he covered her throat with random kisses, his hair caressing her chin. She felt covered with smooth luxury, relaxed and aroused at the same time.

But her arousal increased, her relaxation decreased, as she felt his head go lower and his tongue trailed lovingly over her breast, stopping at the firmed, aching tip to circle and probe. She gave a shiver of pleasure.

"You're not cold, are you?" he asked.

"No." Her voice was low and full. "Eighteen thousand feet and rising."

"Clouds all around us," he said softly, shakily. "I want you so much." He pulled her more tightly to him, nuzzling in her hair.

She put her hand on the side of his face and dragged him back to her, and they kissed again, their tongues meeting this time in hot, deep, writhing kisses.

Once, she remembered, he had asked her to say his name. "Neil," she whispered against his mouth, "you have me."

He kissed her breasts again, working her nipples with a tongue made warm and wet from their kiss, holding her breasts with a broad, steady hand, and then, while she waited, her heart hammering against his chest, her breathing sharpened, his hand covered her lower stomach, his fingers deftly undid the catch of her shorts, and he slipped his hand underneath the constriction of the fabric.

"Darlin', if you'd uncross your legs, I'd feel just like a kid on Christmas morning." His fingers were gliding downwards, spurring and controlling the rhythm of her breathing.

"Happy holidays," she said softly. His fingers began to work a wicked sorcery on her, making her mind spin and swirl. She hardly knew it when he removed the last barrier of her clothing and his. "Yes, Neil, yes." And then the pinpointed, specific attentions of his fingertips ceased, and he placed his two broad hands on her bare hips, holding her up to him, and she waited in a rapt and aching anguish before she felt a low, warm sliding, and the waving tips of the clover and the brilliant blue sky seemed far away, and yet lent themselves to an unimaginable clarity as she dug her fingernails into the small of his back and moaned...

His mouth simultaneously invaded hers, to no resistance, fierce, hungry kisses, random and love-violent, different from the gentle rhythmic movement of his hips as he lifted her, his hand under her shoulders, her blond hair spilling around them over the clover as he searched for, found, and held her most profound and silken depths, covering her face and mouth in fiercely loving kisses, murmuring love words.

She felt a sweetness, as though she were retreating into the chambers of her own heart, the world outside becoming a pulsing membrane. Her hands moved across his back, feeling the smooth, hard, shifting pattern of his muscles as he moved, feeling his breath on her cheeks and her neck like a nectar bath. Her consciousness became taut, a bow bent ever and ever tighter, as her hands moved up his shoulders to find his face and trace it. No negative thoughts intruded, but she had the hazy knowledge that it was the first time she had really touched the face of a lover, looked into the eyes of a lover. His were blue, light-emitting, indescribably tender and pleasure-hazed. Catching her gaze, he smiled at her with a tender half-smile. He seemed overwhelmingly beautiful to her, like a vision. She felt the universe vibrating with love, drifting with ethereal light, with a low, powerful echo which grew and grew as he soothed into her, drawing her back, back, back, until she was released like an arrow into free flight, arcing toward the sun . . .

For an indeterminate time she was aware of nothing, the dream-state of hovering between wake and sleep, when all the psychic clowns cavort on the horizon of the mind in full view, unaware of one's amused presence. And then this state too fell away, and she felt only warm and sleepy, with her muscles and bones renewed and enriched as though the sunlight had entered her and rinsed through her veins with her blood.

Neil held her in a protective grasp, his legs entwined with hers, his fingers playing in her hair, gently stroking back the tangles.

"Mission Control to Kathy Carter," he said softly. "Are you there, Kathy Carter?"

"Come in, Mission Control," she said.

A strand of her hair was caught in a sheen of moisture beside the corner of her mouth, and he pulled it free. "What's new in the stratosphere?"

"Mmm . . . meteor showers. A supernova or two. Lots of little green men and a UFO."

He touched a light kiss to her eyelids. "That was me."

"Was it?" Chuckling huskily, she cuddled her face into

his shoulder. "I thought you looked familiar."

His eyes were bright, raw with feeling. He bent his head to brush her lips with a kiss. "What were you thinking about just now?" His hand traced a straight line down her brow, down the short and tilted length of her nose.

"Just now?" she asked gravely. She kissed his finger as it crossed her lips. "I was thinking—you know, this feeling—it's a miracle. Don't you think more people should know about this? There must be someone we can report it to."

He stroked her cheek thoughtfully. "Well, let's see . . . I have an uncle in Congress. Should we write him a letter? Maybe they could hold a hearing."

"And we could testify or something?" she ventured. "You think anyone would want to listen?"

Neil had begun to smile. "I think the world would be all ears."

"Really? You know how people are about new ideas. Maybe we should keep it to ourselves . . . Do I have a dumb-looking grin on my face?"

"You have a smile on your face that takes my breath away."

"Do my lips look funny?"

"No. Beautiful. Maybe a little bee-stung." A slight frown came into his eyes. "Why, are they sore?" He touched them again, lightly, with a soothing touch. "Did I hurt you, Kathy?"

"No, oh, no. I've just—" She was about to say, "I've never felt like this before," but she blocked the thought while it was half-formed in her mind. She didn't want her thoughts to travel from the present.

"What is it, Kathy?" His voice was gently curious.

"It's . . . it's nothing. I'm sleepy, that's all."

He drew her on top of him, settling her full length on his body. The sun was like a hot blanket on her bare back and legs. She felt cozy and loved as he stroked her body. "Are you comfortable, kitten?"

"Mmmm. I feel so lazy."

"Fishing," he murmured, "will do that to you . . ."

The sound of lapping water floated toward her from the lake. Thrushes and cardinals were a muted chorus in the trees. She closed her eyes to rest, feeling his soft, rhythmic breathing against her cheek.

"Kathy, darlin'?"

She shifted her head, and her hair fell across her face as she sighed into wakefulness. Unfocused moments slipped by. All at once, like a door flying open, her perceptions began to function and she knew three things: that she was outside, that she was naked, and that a warm, nude, and very male body lay beneath hers. She heard her own whisper. "Neil. Oh, my God."

He caught her face between his hands. "It's all right, Kathy. Don't be afraid." He kissed her forehead gently. "Prompt with the residual panic, aren't you? Please keep a few things in mind. First, I adore you. The second thing is, we've both been asleep for who knows how long—and the sun has burned the heck out of your back; I can feel it. So if you're going to try to jump up and run away, please do it very carefully."

"Sunburn?" She looked at him blankly and moved her shoulder under his hand. His touch was still a trail of fire, but no longer pleasantly so. "Ouch! Owww!"

"A very bad case," he said grimly.

She rolled off him and sat up. Her back and hips and the backs of her legs stung with sublime intensity. The clover beneath her bare body scraped like steel wool.

"Bad news," he said, lifting her hair to examine her back as she sat with her knees tucked under her chin. wrapping her long arms around her legs. His voice was grim. "Damn, I'm sorry. You have sensitive skin, don't you?"

Obviously it wasn't meant as a criticism. No one with any intelligence should take it as one. What was the matter with her, that his words should bring hot, hidden tears to the inside of her eyelids? Kathy thrust her face into the furrow between her knees. Thin skin, he should have said. How lame, how utterly lame of her it was to have developed this case of the jitters. She was embarrassed about getting a sunburn, she was embarrassed about reacting so emotionally to the aftermath of their lovemaking; she was embarrassed about being embarrassed. There were only two choices: admit it or hide it. She was too embarrassed to admit it.

"I burn easily," she confessed to her inner knees, then,

raising her head, "but it fades in a day or two. There's no reason for *you* to apologize. Chalk it up to hazards of the great outdoors, and be grateful it wasn't poison ivy. I can't think what kind of story we would've told in the doctor's examining room."

He was shaking out his shirt. "That we were scouts working on a brand new merit badge? You realize, of course, that if our clothes have shrunk—"

"We're sunk," she said, much more brightly than she was feeling. "We'd have to make it back to the cabin zig-zagging from bush to bush. Or raid a fig tree."

Picking grass scraps and clover from his jeans, he said, "I never did understand how they got those leaves to stay on. Just a minute, darlin', I'm going to wet my shirt in the lake, and you can wear that. You'll be more comfortable in something that fits loosely."

She waited under the immense trunk of a tulip tree while he did the chores attendant to responsible care of a canoe and simple fishing tackle. Under the big, damp t-shirt, her fried skin crackled when she moved. Blood poisons from the burn had filtered as a pounding headache and chills in her brain.

Sunburn was a small thing compared to the heavy despair within her spirit. Too late, now, she knew that she had given herself too easily to him, with the unresolved differences between them still stroking the air like wingbeats. Didn't he feel it? No. He was easy and normal, unchanged by having made love to her. He had liked her before, he liked her now. I adore you, he had said. Was that more or less than love?

Staring into high, distant leaves, she wondered at what price she had bought the vivid ecstasy. Yesterday she wouldn't have been able to believe that such a shattering burst of pleasure was possible. He had altered her more in those moments of physical contact than anything else in her life had ever done before, almost as though that gentle and elegantly skillful lovemaking had been some sort of surgery. She felt as though he were inside her still—but in every part, every pore.

After, with David, she had felt little beyond a vague emptiness. And because she had never experienced this kind of height, she was left unprepared for the astonishing strength of the downslide. No! No more! Comparisons were cruel and horrible.

She lay watching the leaves tremble far over her head, feeling the coarse pain of the burned, drawn skin on her back and the liquid warmth that his love had left within her body, until Neil returned and carried her on his back to the cabin—because even the soles of her feet were sunburned— saying when she protested that she wasn't much heavier than a backpack.

Holding him tightly, with her bare legs hugging his waist, she gazed at the bobbing scenery, all too aware of the motion of her breasts against his body, separated from rippling muscle only by wet cotton and the Mad Hatter's tea party. She teased him for a while by laying deep, stroking kisses on his neck, delighting in the feel of his breath quickening as her mouth worked, laughing at the delicious threats he made about the things that were going to happen to her if she didn't stop. By the time the cabin came into view, she was too ill to play and she was grateful to let him put her on the bed, feed her aspirin and orange juice, and spread towels soaked in vinegar and water over her back.

She slept again, waking in an hour to make her way outside to the primitive sanitary arrangements in the little out-house behind the barn. Returning, she sat sideways in a chair, dressed in a soft flannel robe, and watched him make chicken stew with okra in a Dutch oven, a heavy iron pot on four short legs that sat upon hot coals raked forward in the hearth from the fire. Baked apples and corncakes cooked under the ashes. There was no end, it seemed, to the man's talents . . . musician, songwriter, sunburn doctor, mountain man, high-altitude pilot. He was in an enchanting mood, moving without a shirt through the lengthening shadows and firelight, the nearly dried jeans clinging low on his hips, the fabric softly outlining the sensual curves of his legs and his—well, his legs.

His liveliness, his energy, his charm fascinated her, and later—eating his chicken stew—so did his cooking. She chatted with him and joked, never letting him know that they were back to the sophistication contest, and that she had lost, that she was afraid and insecure, that she saw them as strangers who would spend their lives more or less contentedly in different worlds that could rarely touch. But she couldn't ask him for the reassurance she so desperately needed. If you have to ask, it's no good, is it? The one thing she would never become, she thought, was his supplicant.

He washed the dishes in a washtub while she ate corncakes with honey, and then he played and sang for her, stroking magic notes from his battered guitar with graceful fingers, his feet up on the cherry table, his chair tilted back as golden candlelight touched his features in a spectral halo.

It wasn't so awkward, after all, to share his bed. Walking in the shelter of his arm, then watching him draw back the quilt, she said, "The vinegar towels felt great. How'd you learn about that?"

"Hmm? It's an old family thing. Our governess used to put them on my brother and me when we were kids."

"Your governess!" At first she didn't believe it. "Did you really have a governess?"

"I did. Cross my heart." He began to open his belt. "My father says it's the key to my personality. I went into rock music to neutralize my inner conviction that I was an anachronism."

Her appetite whetted for hearing more about his background, she asked, "What was it like—your childhood?"

"An endless succession of shirts with little alligators and boys' schools where you wore a cap and a blazer and played lacrosse."

"Really?" She watched his pants come off. "Is that where you learned not to wear underwear?"

Bright-eyed, he grinned at her, but before he could answer she said, "Did you call your mother 'mater'?"

"I don't recall. I rarely saw her. Now I call her Lillian; that's her first name."

Appalled, hurting for him, taking an instant dislike to his mother, she said softly, "Poor little rich boy."

"That would be the logical assumption." He came to her, resting his elbows with care on her shoulders, standing with relaxed nudity before her, one leg flexed slightly, his fingers picking up strands of her hair and letting them shift through his fingers. "But I'm afraid I'm a lousy candidate for anyone's poster of a neglected child. The immense warmth of feeling between the very disparate members of my family is based largely upon infrequent contact. We get together twice a year, at Christmas and the Fourth of July, have a conference call once a month between my parents, my brother, and me, have lunch when either my father or my mother happen to be in New York the same time I do, and that's it. If we spent the kind of time with each other that your family does—"

Words seem to have failed him at this vision of disaster. Or perhaps it was because one of his hands, traveling slowly downward over her robe, had turned his thoughts in another direction. The other hand began to stroke her throat, just so. Stubbornly, she persevered in asking, "And your brother? What's he like?"

"Umm? Jerrott? He's two years younger. Once in a while we backpack together. He's an artist." Beginning to open her robe, "Makes avante-garde films. He has one— What's the matter?"

"Nothing."

"He made a four-hour film of a guy carrying this decoy duck around Newark into all kinds of incongruous places, talking unintelligibly to the duck. It's called 'You Can't Duck Fate.' Jerrott doesn't come to my concerts and I don't go to his movies."

The robe was gone and he had begun to press kisses on a shoulder she was sure must bear the strong taste of vinegar.

"The thing about your vinegar treatment," she said suddenly, "is that it makes a great contraceptive."

Lying on the bed, he drew her gently on top of him. "If I were you," he whispered, "I wouldn't rely on it."

The deep woods fragrance of pine needles woke Kathy to the blue haze of early morning. She lay partly on top of Neil, their arms and legs braided. She became slowly, warmly aware that he was awake and looking at her. His eyes were soft, his expression gentle.

"I'll bet it's been awhile since you've woken up in bed with a pair of hairy legs," he said.

She thought with a low feeling, trying not to dwell on it, that it was, no doubt, much more recently that he had woken up with a pair of smooth legs in his bed.

"What's the matter?" he asked. "You look sad."

Her thoughts were a jumbled, morning-after confusion. When she was almost ready to speak, not sure what words would emerge, she heard a mechanical roar from the lane beyond.

"Is that a car?" She asked. The engine slowed to an idle outside the cabin.

"A Jeep, I think," he said, frowning, listening. He kissed her on the top of her tangled head and rolled out of bed, pulling on his pants. "I'd better check it out. I'll be right back."

She pulled on a robe from her suitcase, thinking with relief that the worst of her sunburn pain had receded, and went to peer through the curtains. Neil was shaking hands with the white-haired driver of the Jeep, who handed him an envelope before jamming the vehicle in reverse and speeding away, chased by a cloud of red dust. Neil stood in the road, reading the contents of the envelope, and then walked slowly back to the cabin.

Kathy waited for him beside the window. He was tapping the paper in his hand; she could see the Western Union mark on it. A telegram. Finally, with a quick closing of his fist, he crumpled it up and threw it into the hearth, where a few coals still glowed from the night before.

"I've got to go back to New York," he said, the light eyes severe and unsmiling. "Right now. There are problems with the recording I've been working on. What can I say? I'm sorry."

No explanation. O.K. Make the right response, Kath. "Well, sometimes these things happen. It's all right."

He was studying her closely. "Is it really all right?"

Pride was kicking her like a hobnailed boot and ordering her to smile. "I understand. You know what they say about the best-laid plans going astray."

His face relaxed. "Thanks. I'd ask you to come along, but I'll be really tied up, and it would be a drag for you. Listen, there's a little store about three miles down the road. There's a phone there. I've got to go and find a pilot to meet us at the landing strip and fly us to the airport in Chattanooga; I'll put you on a flight back to Wisconsin and catch one for myself." He bent over and kissed her. Again, he said, "I'm sorry, baby."

The noise of Neil's old car had barely vanished when she turned, her eyes blurred with stupid, irrational tears, to go back to the bedroom to get dressed. She saw the crumpled telegram lying in the hearth, six inches from the few live coals. Obviously he had intended it to burn, and she had intended to push it toward the fire; instead, almost sick with craven self-knowledge, she found herself unfolding it. She crumpled it up again and held it on her knee for a minute before, despairingly, opening it and reading it. It was dated the previous day.

DEAR NEIL STOP TODAY WAS TERRIBLE STOP CAN'T MAKE IT THROUGH ANOTHER ONE WITHOUT YOU STOP FEEL AWFUL ABOUT THIS BUT PLEASE COME BACK IMMEDIATELY IF NOT SOONER STOP NATALIE

9

ON THE DAY of the Walworth County Fair, after working for several hours at the Church Ladies' Aid booth, Kathy wended her way through the crowd past fair-goers carrying kewpie dolls and teddy bears, past the balloon toss, past the half-empty Scrambler. In fact, she noticed that the crowd had thinned considerably, particularly of people between the ages of twelve and twenty. She heard the boom of Mike's bass first, and then the music was clear as she paid her two dollars admission and ducked through the flap.

They were finishing a song with a flourish as she entered. Inside, the mystery of the disappearing teenagers was solved—every one of the six hundred seats was filled, with another two hundred people standing at the back, all of them clapping and whistling and shouting for more. Mike and Eric were grinning at each other on stage. Sticks was blowing a bubble, something he only did when things were really going well. As Kathy watched the bubble break into a pink sheath over his nose and chin, she realized with elation that the gate must have been over sixteen hundred dollars—a success! If only they'd had the record to sell.

She scanned the crowd and saw Renee sitting with Fritz

Waller and her father. Renee saw her and waved, and gave her an O.K. sign and a wink. Just then, Sticks did a drum roll and the Firecrackers roared into another song.

The crowd must be supplying some special witchery, Kathy thought. She had never heard the Firecrackers sound this good. Mike's vocals had a new maturity. He was taking chances with more subtle effects, and it was working. Everything balanced, everyone came in at once, and the audience was meeting their energy and feeding it back wholeheartedly. Most of the kids were standing and clapping their hands over their heads by the time the number was over.

Watching Eric and Mike and Sticks bask in the applause, Kathy thought, *I did that.* No, she corrected herself. Neil and she had done it together. They'd done it! For a moment or two, she had a collection of misty-eyed reflections on the value of self-respect, accomplishment, and self-expression for teenagers, and the necessity of providing opportunities for them to happen. Suddenly she wished with all her heart that Neil were here to see this. In spite of the days she had spent worrying about Natalie, she wanted him to know. Their three little sow's ears weren't going to change overnight into silk purses, but after tonight, these three kids were going to have one heck of a healthier outlook on their abilities.

Their setup did look impressive. They had borrowed and rented, and their equipment was cleverly arranged to look like more than it was. Kathy scanned the scene. At the side of the stage on the ground, in among a jumble of guitar cases and unused extension cords, an intent young man she had never seen before was sitting in front of a futuristic recording console wearing a Rolling Stones t-shirt and a pair of headphones, twiddling dials. Where had he come from? A teacher from the reform school helping the boys out? Not likely. She could see over the man's shoulder. The console was too expensive. It made the board at Fritz's look like the equivalent of a Model T.

Sweating and beginning to look pleasantly mussed up, Mike lifted his hand for quiet and began to express the appreciation of the band for everyone who had worked so hard to make this benefit a success. It was a good cause, he said, especially since a good part of the audience would probably be spending a year or two there in the future.

Alarm and laughing protests came from the delighted audience. Mike went on to thank Jill Simpson, their social worker at Walworth, and then Kathy's father, who took a bow to many cheers.

Mike continued, "... A very special thanks to Fritz Waller—" Applause as Fritz stood and waved his Homburg, beaming. "And to Mrs. Kathy Carter, the lady in the back there with the halo and white wings—Hey! Quit trying to crawl under that table, Mrs. Carter. All I can say is that she's some kind of a lady."

From the heat in her cheeks, Kathy surmised that she probably looked like an anemic beet as she mustered the poise to respond with an animated curtsey, shaken and more than a little surprised by the round of applause and the number of people who turned and waved. "And, last," Mike said, "I'm privileged to be able to introduce a man who— well, there's no way to tell you what this men's friendship has meant to us. We're still pinching ourselves. To prove that dreams can come true, ladies and gentlemen, please welcome Neil Stratton!"

Kathy's mind was a maze of buzzing feedback and her heart kicked like a tom-tom as the man who had taken her fishing five days before sauntered through the back of the tent wearing a cotton shirt, soft denim jeans, kidskin boots, and hair that moved when he did.

There was a second of stunned silence from the crowd, then a scattering of applause and a sudden screaming as it began to sink in—the real Neil Stratton, in their little town, at their County Fair! It was common knowledge that he had been seeing Kathy Carter, but the boys had kept it quiet that he'd been helping, as he had wanted them to, out of respect for Fritz's premises.

Kathy's immediate fear was that he would be mobbed, the stage torn apart, and the equipment destroyed. How could it work? But he ran up the steps, went straight to the microphone, and began to talk, and the crowd began to hush to hear him.

Blood pounded so hard in Kathy's ears that she was only vaguely aware of his words. It was his effect that she noticed. He was an expert, a professional, at working an audience. He could garner from them any response he desired—laughter, applause, absolute silence. Just as he would have known how to provoke them into a riot, he knew how to prevent one. He told them about his first impression of Wisconsin when he played Nordic Valley in the spring, and what a great crowd it had been. He'd played the International Amphitheatre in Chicago the night before and what a wonderful contrast Nordic Valley had been. He had said to a disc jockey from Milwaukee—Neil was strapping on a guitar and tuning it while he talked—that if the rest of the country knew about how beautiful Wisconsin was in the spring, they would all want to move here, and then the guy had told him about the winters. A collective groan filled the tent at the thought of Wisconsin winters.

Neil introduced one of Eric's ballads and sang it with the boys. His extraordinary stage presence and vocals gave the words haunting depth. Without pausing between songs, they went into an early hit of Neil's, the title song of his first platinum album, the soft, husky lyrics stroking like mystic fingers through his listeners. They could only have had two hours—less, perhaps—to prepare. Kathy wouldn't have believed it was possible if she hadn't seen Neil with them at the studio, relaxing them in tense moments by launching the kids through hodgepodge, often amusing medleys where "Stardust" was likely to find itself wedged between a pair of heavy metal drinking songs.

Three high-energy songs from the Fifties followed, roaring by like freight cars in the night. Their audience was too busy dancing to scream and too exhausted to do anything but applaud and yell for more when they finished. Neil stepped back to the mike and waited patiently until he could be heard.

"Even in an out-of-the-way backwater like Apple Grove," he said, grinning into the microphone, pausing to receive a chorus of good-natured boos. "Just kidding—there's a lot of talent. In Apple Grove I've met one of the prettiest voices that's come my way in a long time. But the lady's kind of shy, so I don't know if she'll come up and sing with me just on my prompting. Maybe if all of you were to ask her, we'd be able to talk Kathy Carter into laying a little melody on us. What do you say?"

Caught in the radiant nimbus of his charm, they said precisely what he wanted them to say. Kathy felt someone push her gently from behind—she never discovered who it was—and found herself walking forward through a wall of chanted encouragement, applause, and a few good-natured wolf whistles. She wasn't sure what she felt. Blank shock, perhaps. But it was the hometown crowd, her friends and neighbors and classmates, and they would judge her kindly.

All of her senses honed to Neil, cool and lean before her, drawing her up beside him as into a charmed circle, a protected place. There was no time to say so much as "Hello, I was undressed in your arms the last time I saw you." No time to say the words, and yet his eyes, capturing hers, burned that message into her senses.

He looked softly into her eyes and said, "How would you like it if we did 'Let It Be'."

The man with the fancy tape recorder turned out to be a sound engineer and a friend of Neil's, so Kathy's moment on stage was preserved for posterity on a demo tape—"Neil Stratton Live at the Walworth County Fair with Freddie and the Firecrackers—" that Mike and Eric intended to transfer to vinyl and hand over to a local distributor. With Neil's voice on the album, that shouldn't be hard to accomplish.

Half an hour later, Kathy found herself on the Scrambler under the livid glare of fluorescent lights with a vivacious male companion with slicked-back hair, Buddy Holly glasses, and denim coveralls without a shirt, who had smiled delightedly at himself in a mirror before he left the van.

She couldn't say, of course, that no one recognized him. Kathy sometimes saw a passerby look at her, look at him, do a double take, and move off half bent over with laughter, which seemed to delight Neil all the more. The few people who did approach him for autographs were polite and tactful enough not to linger.

And, as it happened, Neil had enough credit cards with him to circle a Cadillac, but no cash. So Kathy had the secret pleasure of paying for hot dogs, cotton candy, the ring toss, and darts while making an outward show of grumbling about it and calling him a gigolo. Generously, she bought him a chance at the dart game, only to have him cheerfully disclaim any ability for that kind of thing, gaze myopically at the balloons he was supposed to break, and then put the dart through the hat of the game's proprietor, who had had the wit to duck hastily. No amount of chiding would make him admit he had done it on purpose, and he was just as bad at everything else she tested him with.

So Kathy, getting fed up, threw three baseballs in a row into a bushel basket to win them an immense toy snake made of pink fur. Feeling her biceps with awe and exclaiming over her machismo, Neil wrapped them together in the snake and took her aboard the Ferris wheel. Suspended fifty feet in the air on swaying steel braces, with his arms caressing her bare shoulders, Kathy discovered that Neil Stratton's sex appeal didn't depend on 20-20 vision and the dry look. Drawing her in to his kiss, his fingers at her side barely pressing the rising swell of her breast, he asked her to come with him to spend the weekend in New York. This time, she couldn't say no.

10

THERE WERE A few quick stops, one at Renee's for Neil to shower, before they took a late flight to New York. Entwined with him in the snake, not as accustomed as he was to late nights, Kathy slept against his shoulder on the plane and in the taxi to his apartment, the legendary Central Park West penthouse.

The penthouse. Somehow, Neil had affected her so powerfully that she had never imagined him enveloped in an environment. Roused gently in the taxi and supported in the loving drape of his arm, she walked through his front door with no preconceived idea to prepare her for what she might find inside.

In the short foyer lined with mirror-back glass shelving that held a remarkable collection of pre-Columbian pottery, Kathy let the snake slip from her waist. Nothing could be more incongruous in this place than a pink stuffed animal.

"Can I get you something to drink?" Neil asked.

"Yes." Her voice was hushed as he left her alone in the living room. She stood turning slowly in place, staring around her like a child in a museum. Hidden light sank from a high white ceiling, melted into muted blue walls, to evaporate among the dark gold fibers of an antique Oushak carpet, an oasis of glowing color on the lustrous hardwood floor. A vast abstract painting hid one wall, a seventeenth-century Japanese screen pleated its way across another, and, to her left, the milky strands of city lights hung in black air beyond an immense glass pane. Behind long couches upholstered in bone-colored worsted wool with silk throw pillows, a tree-sized fern with translucent leaves shimmered daintily, and on a glass-and-bronze table, high-necked crystal vessels bore stems of varicolored day lilies.

Looking around her, Kathy wondered how she could have forgotten that every minute with Neil was basking in an illusion. She was trying on a dream for size, half the time knowing she was overdressed. It couldn't continue forever this way—this long-distance, jet-dependent relationship. But wasn't that what she wanted with Neil—forever? She was astonished by her own capacity of ignoring the serious issues with Neil—or perhaps by his ability to distract her from them. He left little to chance.

Was it chance that he had taken her first to his cozy cabin and rusty car or was it because he sensed that she would accept him more readily there? What a desperate thought, to imagine he might have planned what had seemed so spontaneous and open to her.

She wasn't sure what had reinforced the dormant distrust. Part of it was the vision of him on stage, drawing so many at once under his glittering web, his power over them for that moment absolute and almost mystic. It had seemed wonderful then, but the aftertaste surprised her with its strange, nearly bitter tang. He was too good at it. Too good.

She realized rather abruptly that he had returned. He stood beside the huge canvas as he studied her, and she saw, with a sense of shock, that he seemed to have absorbed the trend of her thoughts. His eye color reminded her suddenly of the hot pale blue of electrical sparks. He must have kicked off his shoes in the kitchen, because his feet were bare as he walked toward her, the sound inaudible. Without saying anything, he handed her a stemmed glass of Belgian crystal filled with ice and a sparkling liquid. Kathy stared down into the glass, watching the flying dance of carbon dioxide bubbles.

"If you drink it quickly," he said, "you won't even taste the crushed Quaaludes."

She raised her eyes slowly to his face. Neil's eyes, hard at first, became softer, and Kathy wished she could see her own face, see what had been there to anger him, and what, after that, had banked the anger.

"I think I'd do almost anything to keep that expression from appearing on your face," he said. "What have I ever done to make you think I could harm you?"

Nervous confusion must show as fear on her face. Were the two that close to each other? She knew he didn't really believe she was afraid he had drugged her drink, but she took a defiant gulp of the lime-tinged mineral water anyway.

"Heck," she said too brightly, "you've got me wrong, chum. I'm afraid to make a move for fear of sloshing something on the upholstery. I haven't seen a darn thing yet in here that looks like it'd go in the washer."

He stepped back and sat on the smooth couch arm, regarding her coolly for what seemed like a long time. "You knew I had money."

"Heavens, have you heard me complaining? I'm just curious about who changes the day lilies."

"My housekeeper." He took a long drink in a way that told Kathy there was something more potent in *his* glass than mineral water. Then he got up again and walked to the mantel, settling easily against it in a loose-limbed way, the carefully cut hair catching the tilt of his head, one knee bent, his arms crossed above the line of his waist. "My luck," he said, "that I have to fall like a ton of bricks for a Wisconsin populist and the *last* woman in the country whose mother didn't tell her it was as easy to fall in love with a rich boy as a poor one. Pardon me if your reaction doesn't startle me into a dead faint. I've known for weeks that once you had to confront the blunt visual evidence of my bank account, there was going to be trouble. Hell, I don't know what kept me from rushing in to throw a cover over the Picasso."

The climate-controlled air felt slightly chilly on Kathy's exposed shoulders. "Probably that you don't have a sheet big enough . . . ?"

"Are you trying to talk to me, lady, or play racquet ball?"

he asked, his eyebrows lifted slightly. "What else are you curious about?"

Neil had never hesitated to flip open a Pandora's box. Kathy picked the safest question she could think of. "Do you feel guilty?"

"About the money? Sure I do. Sometimes."

"And that's why you give away so much it? To assuage your guilt?"

"Charitable contributions are tax deductible. My conscience doesn't assuage that easily. I don't want to learn to live without my guilt. I don't like what happens to people when they succeed in that." He raked back his hair with a long-boned hand, his shoulders shifting against the mantel. "I'm used to women adding me up on their pocket calculators, darlin'. I'm just not used to having the money count *against* me. Let's get down to specifics. How much of it do I have to get rid of to meet your standards for eligibility in the human race?"

Taken aback, Kathy said, "Please?"

"You look at me, you see a record jacket. Have you got any idea how hard I've had to fight to let you know that I'm a man, not a media mirage? I'll simplify it for you. Which part of the money do you object to the most—the part that I inherited, or the part that I earned?"

Treated without a buffer to the full force of that autocratic controlled temper, she could hardly focus on the subject. "I object," she retorted tersely, "to the part that buys you sofas that are too fancy to sit on."

He gave her one of his ironic looks. "Then the sofas go. If I have them redone in herculon and carpet wall-to-wall in nylon shag, do I become worthy?"

Standing awkwardly silent, clutching the slippery glass in both hands, she knew why she had left the hard problems untouched. Neil's insights were too direct to meet safely, and his words, though not designed to wound, could sting like wasp bites. Most men fought to win; Neil Stratton fought to learn. He had made it clear that he knew sofas weren't the issue. All right, then.

"What must I seem like to you?" she asked. Finally, she let her own temper snap. "You can pretend until doomsday that you don't think anything external affects our relationship—not your money, not your upper-crust background, not your fame. And where will that get us? You've guessed how your status affects me. How does it affect you?"

"What do you mean, my *status?*" The last word was acid. "No, don't bother to explain. We've flipped our analytical systems backwards from Victoriana to the Middle Ages. Lord of the manor and peasant girl. You want to know how I see you?"

"Yes."

He took another drink from his glass, his gaze assessing her, his eyes steady. "That's one loaded question, lady. I'm not sure we're ready for that much honesty." Another moment or two passed before he said, "Anything for the lady with the beautiful shoulders. But if we're going to play twenty questions, I don't want to be the one taking all the risks. If I tell you the truth, then I get to ask you a question back. Agreed?"

Recklessly, needing desperately to know what he was going to say, she nodded.

Acknowledging her response with the slight incline of his head, he walked toward her slowly, setting down his glass, and stood close enough to touch her, his startlingly bright gaze wandering lazily over her face. "The truth," he said, "is that I don't like to acknowledge myself as having any 'droit de seigneur' attitudes toward women, but—in honesty—if I thought it would have worked, I probably *would* have tried to buy you." His fingers closed quickly around hers and brought her glass to her lips. "Wash down your gasp of horror, darlin', and remember that you asked."

When she'd taken a sip that had difficulty making its way down her stiff throat, he lifted the glass from her nerveless fingers and set it beside his own. "If you hadn't been so offended by that ridiculous vent fan...I tried, I really *tried* to figure out a way to make it palatable to you—invest in your business, put a hundred thousand in a Swiss account in your name. Anything that would give you the financial security to leave your shop enough to be with me. I want you so damned much, Kathy, that I'd do almost anything to make you mine." His hand lifted gently to support her cheek. "Kathy...lady with the sunlight hair..."

Resisting the hypnotic stroke of his thumb on her cheekbone, she said sadly, "What I let you do isn't much better. When I think of the money you've spent on my plane fares, for example . . ."

His thumb moved to rest on her lips, quieting her tenderly. "That's nothing. Just transportation. Some men pick their ladies up in cars. I have to use a Lear jet. It's only a matter of distance. Now," his hand moved from her face, "it's your turn. Why didn't you ask me about Natalie?"

Kathy felt her stomach lurch, as though she were back in the Checker cab on the Tennessee hills. "How did you know I was worried about that?"

"You were withdrawn when I came back to the cabin and it took three days for it to occur to me that there might be more to it than surface things. Of course you read the telegram. Who wouldn't have? You're welcome to my mail any time. And I don't know what was going on in my head, not to have given you more of an explanation. God knows what you must have thought when you saw that cable, but Natalie's the wife of an old friend I've been working with on a recording. I can't remember the exact text of the telegram, but the thing that accounts for the melodramatic tone is that the sessions haven't been going well, and Natalie's pretty burned out."

Kathy wanted to bury her face in his chest and cry, with relief and shame, but her emotions were too raw to permit an unrestricted flood of feeling. She put up her chin and said with cold formality, "I had absolutely no right looking at your telegram, and even less reacting to it. It's hardly as though we've made pledges to each other of eternal fidelity."

"When we took each other in the meadow, wasn't that a commitment?" he asked, his voice husky, his expression quizzical.

As the hot-cold flush spread over her cheeks, Kathy felt the long-damped anger pushing its way to the surface, a seed edging a tendril through sand. "Why? Is it your custom to have 'commitments' to every woman you're with, Neil?"

The light, quick intake of his breath and the subtle narrowing of his gaze told her that, while he might have been expecting her to ask that question sometime, it was not now. But now was when she needed to know. "How many, Neil? Were you committed to all of them? How many? Ten?" His expression, for once, was enigmatic, as though he was destroying each thought as it began. "Not ten? Then fifty? A hundred?" She could hear the sharp sound of her own breathing in the intense quiet of the beautiful room.

It seemed to take him a long time to decide how he would answer her. Finally he said, "Not that many."

"Well, then, *ninety-nine?* What's the matter? Have you lost count?"

"I don't keep count," he said, slowly, softly. "But if you've got a compulsion to agonize over it, I'll make you a list—names, dates, positions... But why? None of it's worth a second's unease, darlin'. There's been only one lady who could make me walk on clouds while I was loving her, and that's you, love."

She wanted to believe him so badly that the depth of it terrified her. "How much did you care about the others? What were they to you?"

"I meet a lot of people. Some of them become friends. Some of my friends are women. Some I've slept with. Popular wisdom aside, it doesn't have to ruin a good friendship. I can't deny that I've done my share of playing, but I didn't know I was going to find you, or that you'd be as sensitive and vulnerable as you are. You still don't believe me, do you? How can I convince you? Here, let's try this."

He picked up her hand and, after impatiently pulling his buttons apart, slipped it, palm down, into his shirt, and laid her fingers against his chest. She felt the warmth of his skin, and, as he held her hand there, the increasing pace of his heartbeat.

"Physical evidence, lady. You do that to me. You and no one else."

Her own pulse fluttered like a snowflake in the wind as he released her hand and took her shoulders, covering them in long, unsteady sweeps.

"I love your eyes, Kathy darling," he whispered. "They're truthful, innocent. They don't know how to hurt." His lips found her, touching her nose as they moved in a light murmur over her skin, tasting, testing, until he found her mouth, and then covering her lips with a deep, hungry kiss. Kathy's palm, imprisoned still against his chest, felt his heartbeat soar.

The kiss ended abruptly as he dragged his mouth away, his eyes stunningly bright. "Let's relieve the overcrowding.

All my past lovers are going to exit." He pulled open the door to the foyer. "But we don't want them hanging around in the front hall." He dragged from his pocket a leather folder of credit cards and a key with a Chrysler emblem on the stem and tossed them onto one of the glass shelves in the foyer. "So we'll send them out to dinner and the movies." With a self-mocking grin that tugged at her heartstrings, he added, "They *especially* like the credit cards. Who knows? We might not see them again for weeks. That takes care of my ex-lovers. What are we going to do about yours? There was only one, is that right?"

Through numbing lips, caught in an odd feeling that she was dreaming this, Kathy said shakily, "Right."

"One. But, as they say, less is more. We have to be a whole lot nicer to yours, because he was more important," Neil said. "I can't just usher him out. I've tried that already, and it doesn't work."

"Neil . . ."

"Do you think he'd like to listen to records?" She was shaking her head, a slow, helpless gesture. As though she'd meant to answer his question, he said, "No, I've got it. The Yankees played a televised doubleheader tonight and I have it on video. We'll make him so comfortable that for one night Kathy Carter won't have to worry about him. I'll be right back. I'm going to make him a sandwich."

She followed Neil with quavering bewilderment through a doorway and leaned against the door frame, gazing into a kitchen of exposed brick surfaces and Dutch ceramic tile where Neil was slicing rye bread. "Does he like mustard?" he asked cheerfully.

"What?"

Pulling pastrami and romaine lettuce on the rye bread, he repeated patiently, "Mustard—does he like mustard?"

"Yes," she faltered, "and pickle relish."

He pulled mustard and pickle relish from a cupboard and added them to the sandwich, then fished in the refrigerator for a bottle of beer from a Milwaukee brewery. Carrying sandwich plate and beer in one hand, he pushed open a pair of folding doors to reveal a small room lined with book-shelves, the diamond lights of the New York skyline twinkling beyond the bay window. He set the sandwich and the beer on a small stand beside the easy chair, flicked on the big-screen color TV, and placed the automatic control by the sandwich. Yankee Stadium filled the screen as Neil drew a huge floor cushion to the front of the easy chair and invited the absent occupant to put up his feet.

Kathy was not aware that her eyes had released the single, sparkling teardrop until she saw its cool sheen on the outer curve of his finger as he touched it away. The clever face, with its smile lines and spare angles, was richly compassionate.

"I loved him for so many years." Her whispered voice broke on the last words. Absently then, she said them again. "So many years."

He came to her and held her. "I know. Kathy, I know. And if part of him is still inside you, I can love that part too. He and I are working on a reluctant friendship."

Penetrating warmth from his body had begun to dry her damp eyelashes. Gruffly she said, "Just so you don't expect me to make friends with *yours.*"

Laughing huskily, he turned up her chin to look at her face. "Good. You won't find me complaining if you direct all resources at me, forsaking all others. Not that I think that's likely." He dropped a light kiss on the top of her head and his mouth lingered there for a very long time, an eternity. "I'm afraid, darlin', that I've been irresponsibly ignoring my answering service all day. Want to come and sit on my lap while I check in? It'll probably take about twenty minutes."

She gave him a weary, fleeting smile. "Thank you. But does this palace happen to possess a bathtub?"

"Bathtub" hardly seemed to suit the lavish creation in warm terra-cotta tilework that dipped into the floor like a pond in a room where it was the only fixture, adjacent to Neil's bedroom. Kathy spent nearly five minutes figuring out how to set the elaborate whirlpool and temperature controls before she sank into the deep, bubbling waters under rich, flattering light that came from back-lit stained glass panels in colorfully whimsical designs. And when Kathy experimented further with the myriad controls, soft music meandered forth from invisible speakers.

Drying herself in a bath towel from a heated towel rack, she walked into his bedroom, an exotic cavern with walls hung in dark earth-toned natural fabric and a bed covered in a woven tapestry, where spotlights picked out living greenery and primitive sculptures. Her first thought was to slip into her nightgown, and she picked the garment from her suitcase, endeavoring to imagine herself walking around his living room in her terrycloth bathrobe, or waiting on his bed, clothed demurely in pink cotton. She had no business owning this residual prudery after Tennessee, but prudery didn't wait for an invitation.

"When it comes to the sexual revolution," Kathy informed her pink nightgown, "I'm a raw recruit."

She felt the corner of her mouth quirk and then relax into a natural smile. Much of her earlier tension had left her in the bath and now, still a little unstrung, she decided that, foolish or not, she would put her clothes back on. The suitcase, sitting on the floor, was not in a good position for rummaging, so she lifted it and set it on the bed. To her surprise, instead of firmly supporting her bag, the mattress billowed like partially set jello.

A water bed! Woman of limited adventure that she was, she had never encountered one before. A silly grin came to her face as she flounced on to the bed and felt it gently toss her back up again, discreetly sloshing.

From the far room, she heard a sound that might have been a phone hanging up, so she stood up hastily, struck with the ghost of a notion that it somehow lacked dignity to be discovered bouncing nude on Neil's water bed. She grabbed for an undergarment. Her scrambling fingers found the folded silk of an amethyst teddy she sometimes wore under pant suits and she slid into it, tying the laced center bodice, and untwisting the thin ribbon straps on her shoulders. Just how much dignity was there in being discovered throwing on clothes in fevered haste? A quick scuffle through the suitcase failed to turn up her bathrobe.

With no plan in mind beyond the desire not to be found standing beside the bed in some comical state of embarrassed disarray, Kathy ran through the doorway. She had no particular reason for sitting down beside the pond bathtub, but she did anyway, kicking her legs in the warm moving water. Probably, she thought with weary resignation, her degenerated brain was simulating the idea that she was in a bathing suit beside the over-chlorinated outdoor pool back home.

"Kathy?" Neil's voice came from the bedroom.

"In here," she said. He appeared in the doorway, one hand resting on the frame. The day, with its joys and trials, faded quietly, and she was aware only of rippling music and water, and of him. The teddy clung in damp patches to her skin, and she could feel her breasts swelling with gathering sensitivity against their sheer lacy confinement.

"Here I am, overdosing on luxury," she said, raising one leg in a little kick that curtained her foot in a fountain of sparkling water gems.

Neil came to her side, dropping neatly beside her fully clothed to let his legs dangle near hers in the bath, the babbling water darking the soft denim of his jeans and molding them to the curving musculature below his knees. His shirt, untucked and unbuttoned, brushed against her hip as he turned to meet her eyes.

"I must say," he said, smiling, "the right girl will do wonders for the plumbing."

Beginning to bask and soften all over in the sleepy, observant gaze that banished shame, she leaned back slightly, letting her palms carry the weight of her shoulders. "You don't like your big, fancy bathtub?"

"It wastes water," he said, "and I like showers. This is what comes from saying, 'sure, anything' to your designer and winging blithely off to tour Europe." As the images of untold orgies began to vanish thankfully from Kathy's mind, he added, "You'd think I'd have learned my lesson after the time four years ago in Los Angeles when a 'sure, anything' and a three-day trip to Vegas got me a squash court. But maybe—" a scattering of shining droplets of water quivered on her rosy thighs, and with one fingertip, he touched her there, beginning to spread the pliant moisture in a lazy, widening circle—"maybe I should take you to L.A. and set you on the squash court for a while. It would probably start to—" his lips made a feather touch on the side of her face— "grow on me.'

His open cuff fell back on his forearm as he brought up a hand to her throat and his lips captured hers in a light, teasing kiss. His lips were firm and cool above hers, but her hands, catching the open sides of his shirt, could feel the rising warmth of his body against her fingers. Her hands slid slowly lower, loosening the folds of his shirt, dropping to his lap, where taut denim revealed every smooth line, every curve. Moving upward again, leaving the low-slung jeans, her fingers made heady contact with the tight, supple flesh that banded his hips, his waist, his lean stomach. A sigh that mingled despair and need whispered from her, and her blindly searching arms encompassed his shoulders. The movement lifted her breasts, pressing the soft, eager flesh into his body, and she felt the sudden quickening of his breath, the delicious sway of his body into her inviting pressure.

Their kisses were a poignant, dizzying contact, jeweled with his whispered love words. His hand worked gently at her waist and then just under the upwardly thrusting cup of her breasts until at last, rigid with aching, she grabbed his wrist and dragged it up to cover her, opening her mouth to him, letting her tongue slide to heat his lips as the edge of his thumb began its obedient caress of her nipple, rubbing the daintily abrasive pattern of the lace into her sensitized skin.

Her fingers made a shivering trail upwards, catching silken handfuls of his hair, feeling its thickness and warmth slide through her spread fingers. Her lips sought his eyebrows, his short full lashes, the fine angle of his cheekbones, luxuriating in the rich male sensations of him, loving him with such deep certainty that each breath she drew quailed like a flame. The adoration she had never spoken she gave him now with her body, pressing herself into his hands, his name a single slurred syllable as it passed like a prayer through lips rouged from the bittersweet urgency of her desire. It had been no easy thing for her, this rapid giving of herself into his keeping, fraught as she had been with unhealed doubts, yet doubts became nothing under the sensual worship of his hands and the maddening games his lips were playing with her ready flesh.

His hand glided to her thigh, gently kneading the slim line of her muscle, and she felt herself being scooped lightly upward by the hard lift of one strong hand beneath her and the gentle search of the other as his fingertips entered the scalloped lace that hugged her thighs.

"Lady," his voice came, a muted breath-song, tickling her ear and stirring the soft tendrils at her hairline, "tell me you want this as much as I do. Tell me, darlin'..."

"What do I have to do?" she asked, her voice huskily

sarcastic, with a sweet effervescent flutter, as she covered his throat with love nibbles. "What do I have to do—*melt?*"

"Yes, darlin' . . : melt," he whispered, dragging her closer, his mouth burning a tender passage to her nipple, taking it lightly into his mouth through the slippery fabric. His breath moved in hot chilling waves against her flesh through the dampening silk. "Melt into me . . ." His fingers tugged gently at the ribbon that held her bodice closed until it fell open under his hand. He brushed the fabric back until her breasts lay bare to the quest of his mouth, her flesh achingly tight and tender, absorbing the subtle motions of his tongue in heated pulses.

His lips wandered lower, over her belly. "Love, how do you always manage to taste so . . ." catching his breath, "so good . . . Darlin', come against me," he murmured huskily, "just a little. I want—Ah, God, don't stop!" The words were wrung from him with a soft moan as her mouth rained tiny nipping kisses into the nerve-rich flesh at his nape. His voice, when it returned, was a shivering whisper. "Angel, I want to take this off you. You're so pretty. I want to kiss you everywhere . . . everywhere, can you . . . ? Yes . . ."

His lips seared every inch of her flesh, making her so open to him that love filled her like a clinging mist. In a haze, she felt his fingers in a gentle, intimate exploration that threw her breathing into a series of sharp gasps. His own was no steadier, and a faint endearing pleasure-flush spread over his cheeks and gauzed his eyes as she pulled off the rest of his clothes. Laying her back into the carpet with enraptured tenderness, he said softly to her, "I've been in such a bad way for you all day, pretty lady—wanting you on the—" Drenched in the exquisite rapture of his slow entrance into her body, she saw through her haze that his eyes had drifted closed, his face heart-robbingly young above her in its unrestrained passion.

Adoration, without limit and timeless, flooded her veins like heavy syrup and her voice was thick with it as she said, in soft panting breaths, "You—wanted me on the what?"

"On the Ferris wheel," he whispered, "and on the Rock-o-Plane . . . Lady . . . lady . . ."

Breathing deep to find the oxygen to speak, she murmured, "But didn't you want me on the Scrambler?" and then began to laugh, a delicate feast of sound.

As he opened his eyes, the corners of his mouth lifted slowly in a diffuse, blurred smile, "When you laugh," he said weakly, his voice rough, "it feels...interesting. On the Scrambler, all I could..." he had to stop to breathe, "think about was your long, lovely legs, and having them on either side of me..."

But his last words were muffled against her lips as her hands had wrapped around his shoulders, pulling his face closer. "Will you be quiet, Stratton?" she whispered giddily into his mouth. "Do you want love, or conversation?"

Much later, when she lay cupped into his body, his hand tracing the curving hollows of her body, she said dreamily, "You didn't tell me you had a water bed."

His tongue was lightly caressing her earlobe. "Didn't I? That's probably because I don't think of it as 'the *water* bed' any more. After having it ten years, it's just 'the bed'...well, after eight years—the first one grew algae. If you don't think you'll like it..."

"I didn't say that." Then, rather bashfully, "what's it like to—"

"To—to make love on it? It's very pleasant. Much undulation." His lips began to nuzzle at her throat. "Give me a minute. You'll find out first hand." She turned slightly, letting her arms flow over his bare skin. "Maybe thirty seconds," he said hoarsely. And as her hands tightened on his back, and her lips sought his, "Maybe ten...or, better, five...four...three..."

11

WAKING IN THE morning in the light, protective circle of Neil's arms, Kathy heard him draw a long sigh, and say in a voice of husky contentment, "Last night was the first time I've ever seen my water bed get whitecaps."

Dancing on air, she let him take her to a small restaurant where gentlemen in tuxedos served them pink grapefruit juice and French toast with red currant sauce for breakfast. It wasn't until they were outside under the candy-striped canopy that Kathy had her initial feeling of unease when a short man in a tweed coat flashed out of the shadows to take their picture. A commonplace occurrence for Neil, no doubt, because he responded cordially, called the photographer by his first name, and only remarked casually to Kathy, as he held open her car door, "Newspaper."

She had never been to this city that more than any other in the United States meant metropolis, and he had planned to take her sightseeing, but somehow they had ended up back at his apartment, tangled in each other's arms. During the afternoon, still in Neil's bed, they watched a first-run movie on a wall that collapsed magically for the purpose.

As he dipped grapes in champagne and fed them to her, he told her regretfully that tonight he had a gig.

A gig, to Neil Stratton, was playing to a sold-out crowd at Madison Square Garden. Enwrapped in the warm cocoon of his undistracted attention, Kathy had not tried to discuss it with him. Denial. Riding in a chauffeured car into the building through a drive-in entrance—AUTHORIZED PERSONNEL ONLY—Neil pulled her very close and said, "I don't know how to prepare you for all this—the rat race. As my father says, it's a hell of a profession for a grown-up man."

Backstage was a labyrinth of dirty white concrete corridors, reverberating with the barely smothered thunder of the band that was the opening act for Neil Stratton, and the roar of a vast, hungry audience. Neil, in a tawny brown coat of very fine leather, a raw silk shirt, and tight black leather pants, made slow progress through the busy hallways as knots of people hailed him. The "dressing room" was a stark, bare-walled chamber, the benches and folding chairs in a style reminiscent of early Sing Sing dining hall, the floor space clogged with excited, chattering humanity balancing drinks and food. Small sparks went off in Kathy's brain as she recognized well-known faces in the mob that emptied into the hall to give Neil an exuberant welcome. In her classic burgundy dress, Kathy felt like a schoolgirl among glitter garters, leather fringe, and gowns cut right to the waist.

There was no time for Neil to introduce Kathy to anyone, because quips and greetings passed in a quicksilver, unrelenting flow between him and the myriad people competing for his attention. Even if there had been time, a flurry of hurried exchanges would have done little to ease her feeling of awkwardness. There was a peculiarly haunting pathos in standing in the drape of a man's arm being ignored as though these attractive strangers were so accustomed to seeing another unknown female beside Neil that they accepted it without the blink of an eyelash. Kathy began to develop the sensation that she was becoming invisible. She could feel Neil's hard length through the side of her body, but still she was fading . . . fading . . .

Kathy watched Neil's famous bass guitar player, Bobby Rowen, as the tall, swaggeringly lean Britisher exchanged animated and affectionate greetings with Neil. Instead of yielding the floor afterward, Rowen shook his wavy mane of reddish-brown hair back over his shoulders and smiled at Kathy from under a drooping Zapata mustache. She felt herself begin to rematerialize under his friendly gaze.

"Who is she, Neil?" the guitar player asked. "And why are you mashing her under your arm like some kind of a bloody octopus?"

Neil's arm relaxed its hold slightly. He bent enough to brush her cheek with his lips and the touch moved through her like liquid gold.

"Because she and I are going to be Siamese twins," Neil said. "Tomorrow we're going to see about being surgically attached. Kathy, I want you to meet—"

"Neil!" The woman who appeared in the doorway was every bit as tall as Neil and reed-slender, her alarmingly short-cropped blonde hair throwing intense emphasis on her lustrous brown eyes. Her ears were double pierced to hold one silver and one gold earring in each, and the thin satin ribbon tied around her neck dropped its long tails into softly freckled bare skin revealed by her brown velveteen blazer that had nothing underneath. The hand held a smoking cheroot and, as she strode forward through the parting crowd to envelope Neil in a heavy embrace, Kathy saw a pansy tattoo on the girl's wrist. It was the same pansy Kathy had last seen on a piece of heavily scented stationery on a winding Tennessee road. She drew the obvious conclusion that this must be Bobby Rowen's wife and Neil's good friend, Sandy, although it was hard to imagine this person packing Neil whole wheat sandwiches.

Ruffling Neil's shining hair, the tall girl said, "Hi, ugly. Did you read my letter?"

"Sure," Neil returned quickly. "Tea in socks and flu in Tokyo; party for Bruce in L.A."

Laying two sets of strong fingers on Kathy's shoulders, Bob Rowen twitched her away from Neil, presenting her like a debutante to his wife. "Babe, look—Neil's brought us Kathy from Winconsin," Rowen said.

Sandy's severely beautiful face grew a dimpling smile, though she paused to address her long-haired husband sternly. "That's *Wis*consin, you wetback limey." Giving Kathy a one-armed hug thickly aromatized with musk, she said gleefully, "Have we ever been looking forward to meeting you, Kathy!" The elegant grin deepened. "I can see at a glance you're too good for him."

"She is," Neil agreed, "but I may improve yet. Kathy darlin', I—"

He was interrupted by another stir from the door as a man came in. "Neil baby!" Inspecting the pair of dramatically attractive blonde girls under each of the man's arms, Kathy decided they were either twins or clones. The man himself was a well-built specimen with thinning black hair, tinted glasses, white linen pants, an Italianate blue blazer, and a yellow satin shirt open over a hairy chest strung with four gold chains of various weights. "Neil baby!" the man repeated when he seemed to have satisfied himself that he had captured Neil's attention. "Hey, I'll bet you think I'm mad at you after the crap you've pulled in the last two days—barricading yourself in that penthouse, not letting your answering service forward your calls and not answering the messages anyone leaves for you, missing your photo session and the sound check here, missing that interview with *Time* magazine—which, baby, we don't do unless we're *dead*. And then when I try to see you at your apartment this afternoon, your doorman shows me a notice from you that says, 'Don't let anybody up, and that goes double for Aronowitz!' Cute, real cute. Bet you think I'm mad at you. You're wrong. You were a good boy this morning! Picked us up a little free publicity!"

The man released one of the girls and fumbled in a pocket of his jacket. Behind her, Kathy heard someone say surreptitiously, "Well, will you look at that! Mickey Aronowitz with his hands in his *own* pockets for a change."

Aronowitz produced a full newspaper page, shook out the folds, and handed it to Bob. "There you are. Front page of the entertainment section."

At Bob's side, Kathy had a good view of the page and the blow-up of her with Neil under the restaurant canopy that morning. Wide-eyed, with the wind teasing her dress just over her knees, there she was in black and gray ink beside Neil's photogenic grin over a caption that read, STRATTON SCORES AGAIN. Below, in much smaller print, it said *Rock Singer Sells Out Garden*. The article that followed made coy mention of the early hour she and Neil had breakfasted and referred to her baldly as the "latest entrant in Stratton's model of the month club."

"Model of the month club?" she said softly in wary bewilderment.

Bob had bent slightly to catch her words. "They just mean you look like a model," he said tactfully. "Don't let it bother you. Hell, these guys get paid by the innuendo."

Aronowitz, running a leering glance over her, said, "So is this the chick? Now I can see what's so special about you. Feelin' pretty good, aren't you, honey? Does a lot for a lady's looks to have Neil Stratton bouncin' her around for a couple of days on his water bed."

The chorus of titters and outright laughter behind her died abruptly as Neil said grimly, "Reel it in, Mickey. Your next word may be your last."

"Hey, just kiddin', Neil baby." Aronowitz let go of one of his girls and gave Kathy a big hug, which she stiffly endured. "I'm such a kidder. Hey, I love her, she's beautiful, she's an angel. Look at those eyes, look at that hair. They really grow 'em right out there in Minnesota."

"Wisconsin," snapped Sandy Rowen.

"Well, for the love a— Wisconsin, Minnesota, same difference. Great Lakes, dairy farms, am I right?" He grabbed a pair of glasses and a bottle of Dom Perignon from a passing tray with one hand. "Hey, look, give her champagne. She deserves it! You're a good kid, Katie, I love ya. See, Neil, I'm nice to her."

After the white-hot spotlight shifted, Kathy discovered that the interchange had done two things for her. First, it was a clear demonstration that there are worse things than being ignored. Secondly, it seemed to have elevated her in the eyes of Neil's hangers-on from Nonperson to Squeeze of yet-to-be-determined significance. People began to look at her instead of through her. Some solicited introductions, but she was certain that, except for the Rowens and perhaps Alan Despensa, Neil's drummer, the increasing kindness had more to do with pleasing Neil than any concern for her personally. If Neil dropped her tonight, most of these people would have forgotten her face come sunrise.

The moments that followed were to be among the most cynical in Kathy's life. Under the steady stream of flattery,

Neil's eyes were bright and burning, even if the twist of self-mockery around his mouth deepened in a way that unsettled her. Was it Neil here with her, or just the body gone on automatic pilot while the real Neil withdrew to a healthier void? She had stopped fading, but Neil was growing and growing, back into his legend.

The members of the opening band returned sweating, exhausted, and excited from the stage, and the floor trembled with the subterranean boom of the passionately aroused audience. A saturated towel at his dripping forehead, the lead singer of the group, a young, strikingly good-looking star on the rise, shouted to Neil, "Have we got them ready for you!"

Talk shifted to a post-mortem of the first band's performance as the room swelled with their followers and the air became an acrid fog of partially suspicious smoke.

Through a blinding headache Kathy was trying to converse sensibly with Sandy Rowen about the record industry in Japan when one of Neil's road crew, in a t-shirt that said STRATTON in bold letters across the chest, gave Neil a thumbs-up sign from the doorway.

"You ready to do it, man?" he shouted.

"Sure. Sure." Setting down his third scotch, Neil said, "Bobby? They're finished setting up. Where's Alan? No, never mind, he's coming. Tom's with him, Kathy darlin'—" He had laced his fingers through hers and started to lead her toward the door.

"Neil baby, wait!" Aronowitz wended his way through the crowd, a plate of caviar in the hand vacated by one of the blonde girls. "Wait a minute! You gonna do that TV commercial for the designer jeans outfit? Yes or no—I gotta give 'em an answer."

Neil was leading Kathy down a winding concrete corridor, passing unmarked doors and dingy walls. Without stopping, he called over his shoulder to the man following him, "Mickey, have you been stringing those people along all this time? You know I told you a month ago I wouldn't do the piece. I don't wear them, so I don't endorse them."

"Jesus, baby, you're nothing for me but trouble, y'know that?" Aronowitz said, the caviar jiggling precariously on his plate as he rushed to keep up with Neil. "You're the last client with a conscience I'm ever signing. What's so all-fired wrong with designer jeans?"

"Nothing. You're missing the point," Sandy said, following with an arm around her husband's waist. "Designer jeans are fine. He just doesn't wear them. Why does he need to? It's the shape of the rear end and not the label on the jeans that makes the difference."

"Which is why," Aronowitz explained with highly exaggerated patience, "they want to wrap their pants around the best looking buns in the music business. Look, all he has to do is put on a pair of blue jeans, prance in front of a camera for a couple of hours, and then slip back into whatever he got from army surplus. Hey, c'mon; you know what my twenty-five percent of that deal comes to? You're costing me money, Neil baby."

"Deeply moved as I am by your eloquent plea," Neil said dryly, "the answer is still no."

Catching up to the group, Thomas Manzone, Neil's keyboard player, said, "The man has spoken, Aronowitz. Face it. The famous buns aren't for sale. Lordy! Will you listen to the people? Sounds like all those good folks out there have had their Wheaties."

The arena was a hot, electrified mega-cavern hissing with expectancy as one of the road crew led Neil up a set of steps and onto the blackened stage, the thin beam from a flashlight guiding them between speaker stacks and stage monitors, over cables and cords. Suddenly dense shafts of light shot down from the darkness to find Neil, standing at his ease on center stage, one hand loosely clasping a microphone. From the audience came a roar of frantic acknowledgement that shook the building to its I-beams. He stood without moving, a graven idol, the aura of lights tracing his long body in a thin line of blue flame. Very slowly he raised the microphone to his barely smiling lips and the arena erupted.

Watching from an open passage to the side, her ears aching from the deafening noise, her skin numb with the force of her confused emotions, Kathy saw the man she loved across an enormous gulf. Had it been blindness yesterday when he had insisted that nothing external could come between them? They couldn't just will it away. Not the fame, or the press, or the millions who loved him. Nor the

temptations, or even the physical separation of two people
who lived in different ways, in different places. He hadn't
asked her to come to live with him. But even if he did, what
answer could she make?

Neil and an audience. They were the perfect team, a
symbiosis of energy and talent. Moving across the stage,
every gesture, every turn of his body natural and spontaneous, he led his rapt viewers through a maze of pure ex-
hilaration dappled generously with fun. Only Neil Stratton
could look out at an audience half-weeping in the enchanted
grip of a beautiful love ballad and say, "Anyone awake out
there?"

It was almost to Kathy's surprise when Neil came straight
to her when the band broke, drawing her close in the
crowded backstage passage, putting a towel on her hair to
protect her from his sweat as he rested his cheek against her
head.

"Forgive me, darlin'," he said in a voice that was painfully gravelled from its recent exertions. "I know I smell
like a wet pony."

He didn't. She loved the sweat-drenched male scent of
him, but there was no time to say so as people swarmed
around them, claiming his attention in frenetic sequence.
Neil only let her out of his arms for a moment as one of his
road crew brought him a fresh shirt. In fact, Kathy was still
in the curve of his arm as he started to mount the darkened
stage steps for the concert's second half. At first, she thought
he'd release her at the top step, but as he began to pull her
with him into the open, across the equipment-cluttered
stage, she cried out, "Neil! What are you doing? Let me
go!"

"I want to sing with you," he said simply.

"What? Neil, no! Stop it! Don't do this, Neil. I don't
want—"

"Hush, babe. It's all right. Just remember, the mikes are
very directional, so keep it right up there under your lip as
though you were going to take a bite of it."

She could have gone on pleading. She could have run,
except that an electrician at a control console in front of the
stage directed the lighting, and what if he turned the floods
on suddenly and an audience of nineteen thousand people
watched her stumbling flight backstage? And, yes, the lights

did come on immediately, piercing downward to expose her and Neil to a sea of humanity that was nine times the population of her hometown. What had she done, what had she ever done to make Neil think she could do this? Yes, she had sung with him in Apple Grove in front of the same friends and family who listened kindly to her efforts in Sunday morning church choir. Yes, she had harmonized with him in Tennessee, but this—this— Her overshocked body began to tremble in the hot light pouring down on them. In the storming applause that must surely be mixed with curiosity—what *was* that girl doing up there beside Neil Stratton?—Kathy found herself wondering wildly if her slip was showing. And then she remembered with horror that she hadn't put one on!

"Ladies and gentlemen," Neil said, "I'd like you to meet someone who's very special to me." He put an arm around her shoulders. "My mother."

The laughter was friendly and effusive, but Kathy could hardly hear it, or make sense of the words he said to reintroduce her. She stared, riveted with anguish on the winking dance of dimming and emerging lights that hung from great aluminum frames, while Neil led her through the lyrics of a love song. The stage monitors carried back their voices, sweetly mingled, jarringly loud. Checked tears clouded her vision and clustered in her throat as the song came to an end. She wouldn't have been able to say whether the audience was applauding or throwing shoes as she responded automatically to it, somehow made it clear to Neil that she would not sing another song with him now, and made her way blindly down the steps, tripping on the third step from the bottom and falling into the hastily prepared grip of one of Neil's road crew, where she startled herself as much as her rescuer by bursting into frantic, palpitating sobs.

Hands that smelled of musk and strong tobacco landed bracingly on her shoulders, steering her through crowded corridors until they turned her into an empty room and pressed her into a chair.

Blowing her nose into a roll of toilet paper, since no one could find any tissues, and taking gulps from a Styrofoam cup of coffee, it was ten minutes before Kathy could control her voice enough to say thank you. Sandy was sitting opposite her, perched on a metal desk. The little room around them was a catch-all, cluttered with ladders, brooms, big toolboxes, stools, and numbered crates. Blessedly, it was private.

"I'm sorry," Kathy said. "I'm not usually so— Is this something he does often—drag people on stage against their will?"

Twirling her champagne glass, Sandy gave her a lopsided smile. "To the best of my knowledge, this is the first time. It doesn't look like you took to it like a duck to water."

"No," Kathy said forcefully, "I didn't. It's hard to describe. I guess you could say I'm a person who's more comfortable with familiar things. What do you think this was? An elaborate test to see how well I do in the limelight?"

"My opinion? It was three parts adrenalin, two parts scotch, and one part sheer male insensitivity. He's forgotten what it's like to be shy, if he ever knew. We're dealing with a man here who's been slathered over since the cradle."

"Then perhaps it was a case of putting the new toy through its paces," Kathy said, tossing a handful of tissue emphatically into the garbage trolley Sandy had pushed toward her.

"Or maybe the man just wanted to sing with you," Sandy returned equitably. "Has he done this to you a lot? Made you cry like this?"

"I don't know. I think so. I can't remember. Some of it was my fault, I think. My temperament wasn't designed for the degree of excitement Neil provides."

Sandy grinned. "Yeah, well, it's worth the work of getting used to. He may be a little too used to having things his own way, but when you get to know him, you find out that the man's a giver right to the core. I don't suppose he's talked to you about what he's been doing for the last six weeks?"

Finding it impossible to dislike Sandy in spite of her tendency and that of the rest of Neil's entourage to refer to Neil as *the man*, Kathy expelled a long, shivering breath. Succinctly, she said, "Natalie."

With an expression of distaste, Sandy said, "Rapacious female, that one. But dead loyal to Peter, I'll give her that. Look, you probably won't hear this story from Neil, because he's as unlikely as hell to tell an anecdote that makes him look especially good—natural humility or prep-school pol-

itesse, with him you're never sure which—so I want to let
you on to what he's been up to. You see, Natalie's husband,
Peter, used to play with Neil and Bobby."

Kathy remembered the band well, the exciting group that
had broken up in the mid-Seventies. The press had called
its demise the end of an era.

"Anyway," Sandy went on, "they fell apart basically
because there was too much talent in the same place and
all of it wanting to go in different directions. They never
fought, not even once—Neil's doing—but, oh, my, did
they have some heavy eye contact. Afterward, Neil went
out, rolled up his sleeves, and the rest is history. And Peter
went out, rolled up his sleeves, and shot smack."

"Smack?"

"Heroin. Fried his brain. After years of trying, Natalie's
finally gotten him to take the cure, and the carrot she offered
was that Neil wanted to work on an album with him. O.K.
She calls Neil *after* she's promised Peter, so Neil says of
course, and drops everything to fly to New York to intercede
with BCG, Peter's old record label, to get him a contract—
which they were not too excited to do, given Peter's recent
track record. Then what happens when they get in the studio
to record? Peter's so scared of screwing up his big chance
that he spends four hours out of every six throwing tantrums.
Everyone says he'd never have made it without Neil there
holding his hand through every step. Production costs ran
over three hundred thousand dollars. BCG was furious, but
Neil smoothed that over, too. Anyway, they've finally got
the thing wrapped up, and the end product is so good that
they think it's going to put Peter back on his feet again."
Sandy drained the champagne glass. "They say Neil only
lost his temper once . . . the night one of those kids of yours
got into an accident in Wisconsin, and Peter tried to keep
Neil from going."

Kathy had been ironing a square of bathroom tissue with
her fingers. "I was mad at him when he came. He'd sent
me this—this *mountain* of roses."

"Well, I'm not sure if it'll be any consolation, but that
was sort of an accident," said Sandy. "There's a new kid
on Neil's staff, and the kid's always begging the man for
something to do, so Neil told him to send you roses and
wrote a card to go with them. When the kid asked Neil how

many roses, he kissed his fingers to the heavens and said, 'Two hundred dozen.'

"You know Neil, right? But the kid took him literally. When the thing got smeared all over the press, Neil spent the morning on the phone talking to everyone he knows in the media telling them to lay off your case. You probably don't know this either, but you're the first lady Neil's ever invited to Tennessee. Once in a while he invites Bobby and me down for a couple of days, and sometimes Alan or his brother Jerrott—but that's it."

The sepulchral rumble from the auditorium sounded like the sleeping heartbeat of some great captive beast, but in the hallway Kathy suddenly heard the quick tattoo of running footsteps and Neil's voice calling her name. The door opened.

"My God, you *were* crying," he said, standing beside the door, dripping with perspiration, his husky voice marred with overexertion as though it was scratched with sandpaper.

Without much fight Kathy said, "What do you expect? Neil, you forced me to sing in front of all those people! I almost died of mortification."

"Mortification? He said the word as though he'd never heard it before. "Why mortification? You sing like a Lorelei. I'd jump on the rocks for you in a minute."

"For my voice? Neil, nobody would ever jump on the rocks for my singing. *Because* of it, maybe. Why are you laughing like that?"

"Because," said Bob Rowen, appearing at the door, "he came running up here between overtures when some idiot told him you were crying, and *Neil baby's* just realized that he's left nineteen thousand people sitting back there in the dark." To Neil, with an exasperated grin, he said, "Kiss her, Romeo, and then come back to say goodbye to your people."

Neil had changed and used the backstage showers before she saw him again. She wanted to leave and be alone with him in some quiet place, away from his swarming admirers, but the arms that held her shoulders had the restless quiver of unspent adrenalin. When he asked her if she'd like to go to a party, she only said gruffly, "I s'pose I would. Unless this is one of those shebangs where they sniff cocaine off mirrors and eat raw fish."

Burying his face in her hair, Neil laughed and pointed out gently that the hors d'oeuvre in her hand was sushi, which was, of course,"—raw fish. And about the other thing, darlin'—I've got more sense than that."

"You mean you've never been to that kind of a party?" she asked, skeptically.

"I didn't say that," he said with a teasing smile. "Just that I've got more sense than to take *you* to one."

The party was at the apartment of a wealthy young actress. It was here that Kathy really began to understand the meaning of the word sycophant. One gets too much false glamour, Neil had said to her once, but she had never suspected that her own tolerance for it would be so low. Among the record company people, the promoters, and the people who were friends of friends of friends, famous faces from the entertainment world mingled into the crowd, transformed by a no-nonsense reality into human beings as fully flawed as any other. Somewhere under the lively chatter and the clink of expensive glassware, there were true friendships and genuine smiles, but Kathy couldn't pick them out from the steady stream of music-industry talk.

Neil's trick of pulling her on stage with him seemed to have upped her standing considerably in this strange insider's society, but the speed of the turnabout did nothing to increase her comfort. Born and raised in a small town, she had never experienced this degree of emotional isolation or the sense of not belonging. Many things might impress these people, but success was their golden calf. So it seemed, at least. Bone-weary by one o'clock, she could no longer watch with a shred of objectivity as Neil was pulled around again and again to be introduced to someone's friend, to be claimed and kissed, fawned on and wooed. It was infinitely worse to see for herself the barrage of temptation the world offered him than to have imagined it naïvely from an uninformed distance.

At two-thirty in the morning she was slow dancing with Alan Despensa, trying to pretend that the cigarette hovering from his fingers just beyond her back was hand-rolled Turkish tobacco, and to discipline the part of her mind that was seeking to recollect whether the latest write-up in *Reader's Digest* had said that marijuana smoke could make you high if you breathed it in secondhand. Looking over Alan's wide shoulder, she saw Neil sitting barefoot on floor cushions, talking animatedly to Manzone and his girlfriend, all of them looking fresher than three cherries. The girl had been dancing with Neil earlier. Then, as now, he looked so sexy and engaging that Kathy's breath caught with pure longing.

Alan was holding her too tightly. The sharp press of his pelvis against her soft flesh alarmed her, but he ignored her insistent body-language request to leave a space between them. Tired as she was, it seemed a gargantuan task to explain that she wanted to end the dance without sounding like a prude.

Now why, all of a sudden, had it become so important not to sound like a prude? Was she changing? She thought suddenly of her home. How quiet and peaceful Apple Grove was by this time of night, a gossamer breeze drifting through open windows, bearing scents from the rose arbors and freshly-mown lawns.

"I want to go home," she breathed.

She didn't know how Alan heard her over music and conversation, but he drew himself upright, subjected her to a heavy-lidded stare, and then led her by the hand to Neil. Alan bent to speak in Neil's ear and, though Kathy couldn't hear his words, she saw Neil's welcoming smile change to a look of concern. Within five minutes, they left.

In the front hall of Neil's apartment, Kathy slid her arms around his neck and began rather desperately to kiss him, twisting urgently closer as though their joining bodies could bridge the span between their lives. She felt the heavy rise of his desire, the quickening of his breathing in response to her open need, though he whispered gently, in a ragged tone, "What, babe? What is it? Darlin', we'd better talk—"

But she was too tired to talk, too tired to do much beyond the things that would heat his blood so rapidly that he soon forgot about talking. Even then, with tender conscientiousness, he wanted to lead her slowly through the preliminaries. She tried to circumvent even that.

"No, love, wait," he said, his breath a hot mist on her flushed cheeks. "Please. I might hurt you."

"Neil . . . don't make me wait," she whispered.

The sweetness of their coming together was so intense that she shed secret tears into his thick, soft hair. But even at their deepest bonding, she could feel her dreams slipping, slipping. . . .

She woke in a grid of sunlight that speared the blinds. Making her way over the bed's billowing surface, she found a note from Neil on the side table that read:

Love, I didn't want to wake you. I have to be in the studio at 8:30 to redub a vocal track. Sleep late. If you decide you want to come in later, there's a car waiting for you outside. Weren't we wonderful last night? The singing was good too.

> *Neil*

Kathy's wristwatch read 8:20. She lay groggily back. Her head had no sooner touched the pillow than Neil's telephone began to ring—a soft, preadjusted buzz. She realized with an inner start that this was the first time she'd heard its summons. An answering service usually fielded Neil's calls. She let it ring six times before she lifted the streamlined receiver gingerly to her ear and said in an uncertain voice, "Hello?"

"Well, hello." The voice was male, huskily attractive with a faint trace of amusement. "Is the superstar available to speak to his father? This is Jim Stratton calling from Virginia."

Her stomach plummeting, Kathy said shakily, "I'm sorry, Mr. Stratton isn't here right now. He's at the recording studio." Then, with inexcusable stupidity, "This is the maid."

"Oh. O.K." The amusement deepened in the voice that was an older version of Neil's. "Could I leave him a message? Just tell him I'd like him to give me a call. I'm going to be in town next week and I thought we could have lunch."

She hung up after his pleasant goodbye, closing her eyes and finding enormous appeal in the thought of jumping out the window. The way her luck was running, she'd probably land in a nest of news photographers. Oh, heavens, what if Neil's father had come to the door and she had answered it in her bathrobe?

On jerky limbs, she got out of bed and dressed. As she was brushing her hair the phone began to ring again, but this time she paused briefly to stare at it with horrified fascination. Then, grabbing her clutch purse, she fled the apartment.

Outside the building, the air was blazingly hot, and the sky overhead was a leaden gray. Heat lifted in sultry waves from the top of an American-made luxury car that waited for her at the curb. Its young driver introduced himself eagerly to her and confessed he was the one who had been so awful as to send her that embarrassing profusion of roses. She was able to reassure him with perfect sincerity that she fully understood.

Malfunctioning air-conditioning in the recording studio made the air inside almost as thick and sticky as it was outside. Ventilation aside, this place was a far cry from Fritz's Audio Art, though the plush, well-maintained interior was ripe with morning smells. The scent of hot sweet rolls wafting from a barely opened doorway seemed vaguely nauseating. Kathy felt like there was a rock in her stomach.

Following the receptionist's instructions, Kathy jogged to the left, entering the third door down, and found herself in a control room that bore as much resemblance to the one in Apple Grove as the biplane did to a Mariner spacecraft. The voice drifting into the empty room through an intercom belonged to Mickey Aronowitz. His measured cadence indicated he was reading something aloud.

"... This reviewer in no way wishes to detract from the unique contributions Stratton has made to the music of the last decade, but anyone with discrimination and a sincere wish to protect the consumer interests of paying concert-goers will deplore the trend of bored superstars inflicting the puerile performances of their latest lady loves on an unsuspecting public. Stratton has a stainless reputation for starting his concerts on time and delivering the best and the brightest shows in the business, but last night's actions give us cause to wonder if this much-loved rock hero's ego has grown as inflated as today's ticket prices." Newssheets crinkled, and then Aronowitz said, "This morning's paper. *Now* what do you say?"

Kathy heard the light ripple of piano keys displaced by a hypersensitive touch, and above that, Neil's voice. "Critics criticize. That's their job. My 'unsuspecting public' loved it."

"You need a strong dose of reality, Mr. Rock Star, if that's what you think," Aronowitz came back irritably. "You know what that chick is to them? A hunk of mutton. You know what they wanted to see her for? They wanted to have a look at the kind of hamburger Neil Stratton is bringing home from the supermarket." There was a moment's grim silence before Aronowitz went on softly, "Hey, have I ever complained before about you keeping happy? Your personal life is your own head of lettuce, but when your emotions start takin' care of business, then I gotta squawk. What are you doing to yourself, kid? You're wearing yourself out with this flying back and forth to Apple Core, then disappearing into Davey Crockettsville for days. It was a great angle for a while and we got some good stuff out of it, but now it's just burnin' you out, babe. Case in point: that night that kid out there got hurt and you go flying out there after you'd been working twenty straight hours on an album for that junkie buddy of yours. They had to scrape you out of bed the next morning and you were worth a lead nickel on your own studio time. And now this." There was a slap of newspaper.

The rock in Kathy's stomach reformed into an ice ball as she heard the piano suddenly fall silent. Then Neil said, "Mickey, I want her in the act."

"You *what?*"

"I want her in the act from now on."

"I don't believe it! I just don't believe it! Goddammit, what is this? Some kind of a nightmare? You want her in the act *as what?* What are you talking about?"

"It's very simple, Mickey. Watch my lips—I don't want to have a solo act any more. I want to sing with Kathy."

"Are you crazy? What are you saying to me? Are you on some weird drug nobody's told me about? You can't bring that girl into your act." Aronowitz's voice suddenly became phony-reasonable with barely controlled panic. "All right, all right, a few background vocals from time to time. I don't like it, but maybe I can see it."

"That's not what I meant. I'm talking about a new act, with Kathy doing lead vocals with me. New act; new material."

"Baby, you've flipped your wig. We're talking box-office poison here. Suicide. Why don't you just slit your

wrists? Better yet, mine. You're going to ruin us all with
your infatuation with that girl. It's down the drain with Neil
Stratton over a handful of hair and half a handful of boobs."

"C'mon, Mickey. She can sing." Neil was laughing.
"She's got a beautiful voice."

"She's got a *thin* voice, you lovesick moron. She doesn't
project. You didn't have a disaster last night because you've
got a sound mixer working for you who could make Donald
Duck sound like Luciano Pavarotti. He added mid-range
body and pulled enough off the highs to give her a voice.
Baby, you'll never be able to turn her into a pro, because
she just plain ain't got the talent, and she knows that even
if you don't. Why do you think she was so scared out there?
Can't you look at the situation with a shred of detachment?
You're touring, you've got bloodsuckers dripping off you,
you live like a goddamn king, people bring you water ten
minutes before you get thirsty. So what happens—you're
riding through Wisconsin and you run across a fresh-faced
kid in a little town who has enough moxie not to fall all
over you like you were the Second Coming or something.
These people from these small towns—they look dumb, but
they're shrewd. And I know you, baby. You're bored, she
looks like a challenge, and, before you know it, soup's on.
What I don't understand is why you've let it spiral. You
can get rid of women better than any man I ever met."

When Neil's voice came again, his words were slightly
muted as though he had moved away from the open mike.
Almost absently, he said, "I want her, Mickey. You got any
equations for my future, put her in."

Backing slowly toward the hall door, Kathy could almost
hear Aronowitz's disbelieving headshake. "Neil, Neil,
baby. You've got your head in the clouds. This is a straight
girl. She's not for you, old man. You know what girls like
her do? They forget to take their pills. You get up one
morning and find a summons for a paternity suit in the mail.
That'll wake you up. She keeps you interested today, but
do you want her hanging around your neck for the next
eighteen years?"

But Kathy didn't wait to hear his answer. Because
Mickey Aronowitz was right. She turned and walked down
the hall. It was time to go home.

12

NOVEMBER HAD COME, the early November of fallen leaves
and brown grass, and a burning tang in the air under a bright
blue sky some days; other days, like today, rain-soaked and
chilly. The leaves had turned from the lush green fullness
of late August through September's riot of color. In early
October a cold wind had come howling out of the northwest
one day and stripped the branches down to spears. There
were still some torn-sheeted Halloween ghosts dancing in
the naked elms, and a smashed pumpkin left an orange
smear down the middle of Broad Street, a smear which grew
dimmer with each passing day as cars drove over it turning
in to the supermarket.

The world had turned on its axis. Summer was very far
away. Kathy sat in her shop, taking a break over the tedious
clarinet repair, staring with a sense of desolation at the
vibrantly healthy elephant ear plant that was a bright spot
of green inside a gray window streaked with rain.

Neil had sent the elephant ear plant.

Her thoughts slid back, as they had done a hundred times
before, to the morning she had run away from him in New

York, and to the tear-splotched note she had written that
had left no room for compromise.

> *Neil,*
> *I can see now that you've done everything you can for
> the two of us, but it isn't going to work. Do you remember
> the story about the city mouse and the country mouse? I
> can't change enough to live the way you do, Neil, and I
> can't exist in your world as I am now. Since I'm sure you'll
> figure it out anyway, I'm going to confess that I overheard
> your conversation with Mr. Aronowitz about me becoming
> part of your act. I understand. After I said that inane drivel
> about your status, you wanted to somehow make me more
> secure by raising mine.*
> *I don't know what to say about it except that you're crazy
> in a wonderful way and it won't work. I need quiet streets
> at night, and a sense of belonging, and the feeling that my
> nieces might stop by after school to play kickball with me
> in the alley behind the shop, and that I can walk over to
> my dad's house early in the morning after a heavy snowfall
> and shovel out his driveway. So much for leaving home.
> And I can't go on seeing you sporadically. It will be too
> hard. I can't, Neil. The worry and imagined jealousies
> would kill me. Please don't come or call or write me letters,
> because I can only be so strong. Please.*
>
>   *Kathy*
>
> *P.S. Your driver is terrified you're going to fire him for
> taking me to the airport. Please don't. I made him do it.
> He wanted me to call you first, but I couldn't.*

She had been home three days when the flowers began
to arrive. The first had been a huge, showy basket of impatiens with an enclosed note.

It said: "This is not a letter, this is an enclosure. I'm
going to say it with horticulture. Please direct your attention
to the first letters of each type of flower, which will spell
a message."

I had been for impatiens. A few days later came *L*—
lavender, which the enclosure informed her rather grandly
was a perennial, so she should plant it outside. *O* had been
orchids and *V* was dainty violets with powdery yellow cen-

ters. *E* had been the elephant ear plant with an apologetic enclosure reading: "It was this or Easter lilies, which the woman at FTD assured me were too funereal, at this time of year. She has also informed me sternly that edelweiss was out of the question. She says I'm a very interesting case."

Then, there had been *Y* for yarrow. *O*—Oriental poppies had arrived two days after the yarrow. The last note had said simply, "Flowers don't start with *U*. Enclosed please find one umbrella."

The umbrella, drying in the back room after a trip to the grocery store, was her last direct contact with Neil. For five weeks there had been nothing, except a letter from Sandy, which had ended, "Keep in touch no matter what happens. I like you."

Over the rumble of distant thunder, the little bell over Kathy's shop door tingled as it opened, and Eric Carpenter, followed by Mike and Sticks, came in with a rush of cold, wet air.

"How's it goin', Mrs. Carter?" Eric asked, shaking the rain out of his long blond hair as the three came paddling over to her.

"Oh, pretty good. Getting a little tired of fishing wet leaves out of the downspouts. How're we selling? Have we made the charts yet?"

They had begun by cutting a release of three thousand copies from the master tape made from Neil's appearance with Freddie and the Firecrackers at the county fair. Neil, dealing directly with Mike and the social work staff at Walworth, had given them a check to cover the first pressing and had taken care of the publishing rights himself. The album had sold locally in stores, and then, wonder of wonders, someone in Milwaukee who owned a chain of eight record stores had placed an order for two thousand more. Was it true that Neil Stratton really sang with them? In another week it had become a collector's album for Neil Stratton fans, as well as a regional hit in its own right.

Eric grinned. "Mike got a call today at the school for someone who wants to talk about national distribution. Incredible, huh?"

"Just don't forget that I knew you when," Kathy said, smiling. "Hey, would you guys like to come upstairs and have some hot cider or something? We could dry your coats over the radiator."

"Sorry, your dad's letting us practice in his basement this afternoon and we've got to get back," Mike said. "We just stopped over because—" He hesitated, then set a rain-spotted bag on the counter in front of her. Hurriedly, he added, "Did you know that Neil Stratton is in Los Angeles this week?"

"I—" The faint draft from the front window that needed regrouting began suddenly to penetrate Kathy's Shetland wool sweater. Automatically, she stood up. "No. I didn't know."

"Look Mrs. Carter," Eric said, after he had captured her gaze, "I know you think I'm just a kid and I don't know whereof I speak, but there's a couple of things I've learned from you. You remember when we were working on that first tape, and we used to get real down about a certain song, and wanted to trash the whole thing? Well, you used to always say, hey, don't throw it out. Even good ideas need work. Sometimes you've got to change things around, sometimes it doesn't end up the way you expected it to, but if it's really good, it's worth saving. Like, uh, I know it's not the same thing, between you and Neil, but—" He touched the paper sack. "Listen, open this up when you're alone, all right?"

Sticks opened his mouth as though he was going to say something and, well conditioned, Kathy groped blindly in her pocket for a package of gum. Ignoring with gentle dignity the foil wrapped stick she held out to him, Sticks said, "The guy really loves ya, Mrs. Carter."

Long after the tingling bell had signalled their departure, Kathy stood where she had been, the gum wilting slowly from the heat of her fingers. Then, in a rush that resembled panic, she locked the front door, flipped her sign to read "Closed," and, lifting the paper bag with elaborate care, she carried it to her back room and sat on her burgundy sofa with it folded in her arms. A record, said the shape. Open this when you're alone. . . .

After ten minutes, she opened it. On the record jacket was a photograph of a long railroad trestle in a rural setting, eerily misted to a radiant silver in a shroud of fog. *Neil Stratton: The Black Bridge.*

Her heart doing things that she would have thought were anatomically impossible, Kathy stumbled up the stairs to her apartment, and, through filling eyes, stripped the cellophane from the cover and put the record on her turntable. The title song, "The Black Bridge," was Song One on Side One.

The instrumental piping through her worn needle had an intrinsic beauty, unsentimental yet easy. The subtle internal rhythms captured the imagination with slow but compelling poignancy. When Neil's voice began to sift through, she was too torn with rioting emotions to do more than catch the lyrics in phrases: "Pretty darlin', you were the sweetest thing I've ever opened my eyes on ... why has being strong come to mean goodbye ..." and the chorus:

"You said I was loved by the world,
        but all I ever needed was you, my friend,
Take me back to the Black Bridge,
Let me start it all over again."

She played the song over and over, then picked up the needle and stood watching the turntable go silently around, Sinking in place on her carpet, she put her head in her hands, her palms pressing into her eye sockets, her fingers icy against her scalp. Blurred pictures capered behind her eyelids, remaining as wispy images when she opened her eyes. Looking up through them, she saw the magnetic butterflies on her refrigerator, arranged as Neil had once left them, in the shape of a heart. What had made her think she could walk out of his life?

Kathy gave herself up to the ghosts of another time—to the pungent tang of pine and sweet clover and bone-deep warmth and the hum of honeybees. Hardly knowing what she was doing, she scrambled to the phone, lifted the receiver, then slowly let it drop back to its cradle. No. This time the telephone would not serve her. She had to get to Neil. And for no other reason than that she had to feel the warmth of his arms, hear that enchanting gravelled voice call her name. Kathy Carter, who had always been so careful and conservative, was going to fly to the arms of her lover without plans, without solutions for the future, without anything beyond the simple burning need to be close to him.

Merciful numbness settled over her as she reached for the yellow pages, but a series of phone calls and figures jotted on the little phoneside chalkboard soon told her that she was going to have to take a bus to the arms of her lover. There just wasn't enough money in her savings for a round trip plane ticket, and even in this advanced state of mental anarchy, she balked at arriving penniless in Los Angeles with no route for escape. If only she hadn't used up most of her savings on the moped. She had bought it during the period Renee called "The Mini-Nervous Breakdown Following the Flight From New York."

There was barely time to get to the bank. The teller was pulling down the old-fashioned teller's window when Kathy ran in breathlessly asking her to please wait on her before she closed up. Then, after dashing back to the shop and scribbling a note for Renee, she was riding out of town on her moped through the damp streets, wearing a scarf and a down-filled jacket to ward off the autumn air, her helmet strapped on her head. A couple of hours later, Kathy caught the bus in Madison, after paying an all-night gas station attendant ten dollars to park the moped on his lot for a week.

Sixty-five traveling hours and three sunrises after leaving Wisconsin, the bus rolled into Los Angeles. A snowstorm in the Rockies had made it hours late. Kathy looked out at a vista of concrete and palm trees, awestruck by the spectacle of men and women in shirtsleeves in November. She ached to the eye sockets from travel fatigue and wondered what spirit of madness had prompted her to set out to Los Angeles after Neil without giving him the benefit of so much as a phone call. What if he was no longer here? What if he was here but with another woman?

Riding down the long, crowded escalator from the busport, her jacket knotted around her waist, clutching her duffel bag and moving among herds of hothouse California hybrids, Kathy had never felt quite like such a dairy-belt hick. That man on the bench, with the small brown bag in his hand—was that a derelict? And why was that man with the ring on every finger staring at her?

She went straight to the telephone, dragged the number of Sunrise Corporation from her back pocket, and pressed out the number. After two rings, a recorded message an-

nounced coolly that the offices were closed at this hour. Of
course. It was seven o'clock at night.

Alright, Kathy, be calm. Don't let your imagination run
away with you. The man with the rings is *not* staring at
you. He's staring at . . . oh, God, he *is* staring. So what? Let
him stare. Concentrate. Who else might have Neil's phone
number? Renee. She's talked to Neil several times on the
phone. Kathy hated to call Renee because she would have
to answer a lot of questions about whether or not she was
all right, which would be painful. It didn't seem, though,
as if she had much choice. Swallowing her pride, she called
Renee collect. No answer.

Trying not to panic, Kathy piled enough coins in the
phone to get through to Walworth School. Eric and Mike
talked to Neil all the time. Surely they'd know . . . But at
Walworth, an irritable male voice told her that it was after
hours and the boys weren't allowed to take calls.

The man with the many rings, edging closer to her, was
undoubtedly not as sinister as he looked, but Kathy abandoned her fruitless call and retreated to the ladies' room to
clean up before she tried another call to Renee. While she
was bent over the sink washing her hair under cold water,
someone stole her duffel bag.

Sometimes you're kinda naive, Ms. Carter. The only
smart thing she'd done in the last three days was to put her
wallet and return bus ticket in her hip pocket.

The rest room was deserted. She sat despondently under
the wall hand dryer, letting the blast stream into her wet
hair, and rescuing a copy of the Los Angeles *Times* that
someone had discarded halfheartedly into the trash can beside her. Flapping the pages open on her knee, she found
Neil's face smiling up from her lap. The quarter-page rec-
tangle advertised a concert tonight in Los Angeles. Bingo!
Or, sort of bingo. A little banner running across the bottom
of the ad said: SORRY SOLD OUT SORRY SOLD OUT.

It was not, perhaps, ideal, but another failed call to Renee
showed that this might be her only chance. It took twenty-
seven of her remaining thirty-two dollars and fifty cents to
reach the sport arena where Neil was performing.

Musty tropical darkness hung over the parking lot sur-
rounding the huge open-to-the-sky arena. Perspiring delicately into her quilted jacket, Kathy wished that, despite the

splashing at the sink, she had had the sense not to have taken off her blouse and slipped it in the duffel bag before washing her hair.

She walked slowly around the high outer walls, staying within the oval bleach of the floodlights. The crowds were thicker beside the steps leading to the stage door. Drivers from the line of hired limos were watching beautiful, daringly dressed young women trying to talk the two bored security guards into letting them backstage. They cajoled; they threatened; they told outrageous stories. To everyone, the answer was the same. No one was permitted backstage without a pass. No, they wouldn't carry messages back to the band. What's more, Kathy learned from conversation around the fringes, the band wouldn't use this exit. They drove in and out through a well-guarded underground entrance.

Twin fantasies postured like shadow puppets in her mind. It was either, she realized despairingly, throw herself in front of Neil's limousine or search out the Salvation Army for a place to spend the night. And what if there was no Salvation Army in the neighborhood? Beyond the arena, and its vast parking lot Kathy could see the high wall of a cemetery. Wandering around the perimeter of the arena making a conscious decision not to cry, she thought about how affecting it would be to curl up against one of the cemetery headstones for the night. Hadn't she always expected her relationship with Neil to end like a French art film?

Residual indigestion had kept Kathy from eating all day. Weak with hunger, tension, and remorse, she suddenly felt dizzy. She sank into the dark hollow between two Chevies far off from the crowd. Some day she was going to look back on all this and wonder what had ever possessed her to behave with such eccentricity. Neil, where are you? If only she'd waited at the bus station until morning.

Light patterns moved on the blacktop beside her knees, and she followed the long shallow line across to leather boots, tight black jeans, a black shirt with white fringe, and dark eyes shining dangerously in a strange face. The smile on the thin mouth was the same one the wolf gave Red Riding Hood.

"Hello, young lady," he said. "Aren't you out past your bedtime?"

Her eyes dilating in fear, Kathy started to scramble to her feet, but was pushed firmly back to the pavement by the tall man as he hunkered down beside her.

"Don't run off. I'm not going to hurt you," he said. "What are you doing out here all by yourself? Are you in some kind of trouble?"

Eyeing him cautiously, she said, "I wasn't until you showed up."

"Yeah, well, you'd better be nervous. This is no place for little foxes to be out running around by themselves." The dark eyes were inscrutable as he raked back his long hair with one large hand. "How old are you, anyway?"

"Twenty-four."

He laughed. "C'mon, jail bait. How old are you?"

"Jail bait!" Furiously, she dragged her wallet from her back pocket and showed him her driver's license. "Convinced?" she snapped.

"Well, well, well . . . I never would have believed it. You look like a kid. Wisconsin, eh?" He picked the wallet out of her fingers and casually counted the bills. "This all the bread you got?"

"Yes," she said sourly. "If you're going to steal it, please do, and then *will you please go away?*"

"I don't know," he said, handing her back the wallet intact. "I might in a minute. First tell me what the problem is."

She sighed and put her head back, too fatigued to maintain anything as strenuous as terror. "Who are you?" she asked. "The parking lot social director?"

"Talk to me, baby." It was an imperative.

"If that's the only way to make you go away . . . I have to find a way to get backstage."

The straight eyebrows shot upward. "At a Neil Stratton concert? Impossible, sweetheart. Backstage passes to a Stratton show are like pure gold. You never see them on the market."

"The market?" she asked.

He lit a cigarette and offered it to her, sliding the pack back into his shirt after she shook her head. "I mean," he said, "there's no one who's lucky enough to get one who'll sell it. It'd probably bring you upwards of five hundred dollars if you could get hold of one." He held the cigarette between his lips as he pulled a green cardboard ticket out of his pocket, flipping the face so she could read it. "What you're seeing here is the last ticket in Los Angeles to the Stratton show tonight. Interested?"

"Yes! Yes, I am, but..." Illumination came suddenly. "You're a scalper! One of those people who buy up tickets in blocks and resell them at enormous profits—is that right?"

He appeared to be content with that description. The dark eyes narrowed again into a smile. "Very good. You see, I'd like to find some way for the two of us to do business, but we've got a little problem. Any one of those chicks by the stage door would give me a hundred and fifty dollars for this ticket."

"A hundred and—" Her breath failed her.

"Sweetheart, Stratton could fill an arena three times the size. I'd like to be nice to you, but I'm afraid my principles don't allow me to give things away for nothing."

"I see," she said. "We are mercenary, aren't we?"

"We are *very* mercenary," he agreed, palming the cigarette, the red ash glowing. "Mayhap, though, we could barter."

"Mayhap," she assented dryly, without much hope, watching his dark, meticulous gaze travel interestedly over and down her seated frame, the study seeming to end with her feet. "My shoes!" she said suddenly. "They—they're very good walking shoes. L. L. Bean, you know, chrome tanned cowhide with plantation crepe outsoles."

"There are other assets of yours that I think I'd find a lot more...liquid."

The words she might have misunderstood; the tone of voice, never. Her shock expressed itself in a series of dry coughs. He took advantage of the huffing to pull her to a standing position and begin to lead her down the line of cars with a matter-of-fact grip around her convulsing shoulders.

"My van," he said, indicating a monstrous midnight-blue vehicle with an exquisitely painted fantasy mural of a skeleton galloping on horseback.

The coughing surrendered abruptly to her control. "Wait

a minute! I have a return bus ticket, Los Angeles to Madison, Wisconsin. I think it could be cashed in for value."

Leaning back against a Camaro, smoking, he didn't appear to be upset by her rejection. "How much?" he asked.

"I bought it for one hundred and forty dollars."

"Well, young lady," he said slowly. "It looks like tonight you're going to see Neil Stratton."

Most of the concert had passed before Kathy was staring down from her seat on the high bleachers to the stage, where Neil sang inside a cloud of smoke-blue light. Every moment, every familiar gesture, brought her fresh agonies of tenderness and need. His voice raked like a soft brush over her senses. She came out of her trance to see that the crowd around her was half-sick with wanting him, too. The chant Neil, Neil, Neil, ribboned pulse-like through his songs, and the shouted applause and stomping that punctuated the end of each song had a strong tinge of hysteria.

In the empty no-man's-land that separated stage and audience, security guards paced like tigers, grabbing anyone, male or female, who tried to breach the stage area. Kathy's jacket was like a sauna on the top half of her body as she began to thread her way down aisles filled with clapping, dancing human beings, their eyes glazed over with bliss. She had no plan in mind, except that she must somehow find a way to catch Neil's attention. But that wasn't going to be easy. If only there were a way to get on the stage itself . . .

The thought came to her that if the Firecrackers were here, they would have found some way to get her up there. What she needed was a group of honest-to-golly juvenile delinquents.

She found them seated six rows from the front. She wasn't sure how she knew—prolonged acquaintance with Mike and Eric, perhaps—but these kids' faces had the same quality of rebellion and recklessness. Neil was on the other side of the stage, crooning red-hot harmonics into a mike that must be melting under his fingers, and passed her a note as Kathy sidled up to one of the young girls in the group, and passed her a note that said: *Help, I must get on stage!* It might have helped that Kathy herself looked about seventeen years old in her jacket and blue jeans with her finger-combed hair loose on her shoulders. The kids said yes, all of them happy to participate in any act of rowdiness. With the morose recollection that only three days ago she had been a respectable, conservative citizen with an untarnished reputation for stability and common sense and a strong determination to end all contact with Neil Stratton, Kathy let a muscle-bound eighteen-year-old boy heft her up to straddle his shoulders. Tottering dangerously, steadying herself by clasping his body with her feet, she discovered that any desire she had for Neil to notice her had mysteriously vanished.

Kathy watched the head between her thighs dubiously as it tilted back to receive a long pull from a wineskin and thought longingly about the Salvation Army.

The kids had warned her in graphic detail about the guards. The young man she was sitting on had seen broken jaws, dislocated shoulders, even concussions. The job of the guards was to protect the performers, and they were going to do it. If they caught you going for the stage, you could expect to be carried roughly to an exit, literally tossed out, and not allowed back in. If you left a purse or wallet behind, tough.

Suddenly Kathy's co-conspirators began to create a diversion in the aisle on the opposite side of the stage, where Neil was singing. One of the girls collapsed on the ground, pretending to faint. Security people ran toward her to see what was going on, leaving enough territory unguarded for the boy to rush through and pitch Kathy up the six-foot wall and onto the stage.

She landed with a force that jarred the wind from her lungs. Through a blur of pain she saw that Neil, pro that he was, and accustomed to the odd ways his fans sometimes showed their devotion, hadn't even glanced over. A huge security guard caught sight of her from behind the stage and began sprinting toward her with all the reticence of a linebacker for the L.A. Rams. Kathy rolled wildly across the dusty pine floor and flung her arms around Bob Rowen's leg. He ignored her. Or at least he did his best even though she was banging his kneecap. Finally, in desperation, with the guard bearing down on her, she bit him in the leg.

Then, he looked down. Barely in time, he recognized her, his head jerking back in surprise. He stopped playing and held the guard at bay with a quick gesture and summoning one of the road crew, who bent worriedly to her. If Neil glanced their way to see why he'd suddenly lost his bass, Bob's body blocked the movement from her.

Escorted quickly backstage, her heart beating wildly, Kathy had to endure a five-minute shouting match in the crowded back corridor between Neil's roadies and the head of security, who wanted to give her the immediate heave-ho.

Finally the roadie ended it by saying, "Ah, hell, now look what you've done. She looks like she's going to cry and, if you think that's small potatoes, let me tell you, you've never seen this chick cry!" As he led her firmly away and down the hall, he added, *"Are* you going to cry?"

"No. I decided not to in the parking lot. Oh, please!" she said, seeing that he was about to lead her into a crowded room, identical to the one in New York in its food-and-drink-laden tables and its expensively casual inhabitants. "Not in there."

He looked at her sharply. "Sure, honey. Anything you want. The band shares a dressing room next to the showers. There's no one in it right now, so why don't we put you in there? Hey, look, everything's going to be O.K. Don't freak on me, all right?"

"I'm not going to freak," she said woodenly, not sure what the word meant, but positive that it wasn't something Kathy Carter would ever do. Why wouldn't her heart stop racing?

"Yeah, well, I think you'd better sit down," he said, bringing her into a long, untidy dressing room and urging her gently onto a folding chair. He rubbed her back soothingly with the flat of his hand. "Try to relax, honey. Everything's cool. Look, I have to get back to the stage. You going to be all right?"

After he left, she went to the huge wall mirror to stare at the face that looked like it was going to freak. Except for the nearly suffocating speed of her heartbeat, she felt nothing beyond a slightly nauseating anesthetized tingle in her arms and legs as she examined a face stripped of color, with gold-fringed eyes enlarged like those of a captive doe. After an eternity, she became aware that the sounds of the audience were no longer muffled by music. The traffic of footsteps in the corridor increased. Two tense minutes passed. Then,

from the busy hallway, she began to hear Neil's stepped-up
drawl, roughened from the harsh punishment of his work
on stage. His tone was furious.

". . . Aronowitz maybe, but the rest of you, never," he
was saying. "I want that girl out of my dressing room *now*.
And the next time one of you jokers sees fit to procure a
woman for me he is going to feel every bit of remorse I can
arrange."

"Neil, you stubborn bastard, will you just go in and look
at her?" The English-accented voice belonged to Bob
Rowen.

Seconds went by before Neil said in a low voice, "I'm
going to forget you said that, Bobby."

An increase in the cheerful commotion within the
crowded room down the hall told Kathy that Neil had joined
the party. Instantly, Alan Despensa was at the dressing-
room door, smiling blindingly at her, hauling her into the
corridor and toward the crowded room.

"No. Oh, no," she moaned, balking confusedly against
Despensa's grip. "Don't! He doesn't want to see me."

Despensa pinched her cheek and hissed, "Shh!", delivering her to the threshold. Gazing through the bubbling
crowd, Kathy saw only one man—Neil, with his back to
her, talking to Bobby Rowen, who grinned and struck Neil
lightly on the shoulder, indicating the doorway.

Neil's voice came to her clearly as he began to turn.
"What the devil is it with you?" he said. "There's only one
woman on this earth that I'm interested in seeing, now or
ever, and that's—" His eyes came to rest on her, and their
vital depths caught like kindling. He said nothing for a
moment, and then, very quietly, "Kathy."

They stood looking at each other, the sound around them
fading under the pressure of curious stares. Not moving at
all, Kathy was barely aware of Alan Despensa's arm leaving
her waist. All she could do was drink in the sight of Neil,
trying to absorb him slowly, like a too-potent tonic. He was
standing quite still also, beside a table strewn with discarded
glasses, the light touching the pattern of the blue silk shirt
that exactly matched the pale, extraordinarily dense blue of
his eyes.

Again he breathed, "Kathy . . ."

For a long moment, his expression seemed to her like

a kind of almost wondering incredulity, and then, very slowly, it began to alter. Through aching despair, she saw the gathering of raw anger in those light, breathtaking eyes.

"Lady, maybe you'd like to tell me what you're trying to prove?" he rapped.

Briefly, the nausea became so strong that she had the panicked thought she was going to be sick. Then her own anger arrived, galloping to answer his.

"*I'm* not trying to prove anything, Stratton. Tonight is the last time I'm ever going to risk my neck jumping onto any stage you're on."

"Thank God for that!" His warmly furious gaze abandoned its intense contact with hers, traveling over her with unmistakable anxiety to take in the details of her appearance. The survey ended irritably on her bright red jacket. From his expression, she would have thought wearing it was worse than all the rest. "And what the hell are you doing in a heavy ski jacket?" he snapped. "It must be eighty-five degrees in here. Are you trying to develop heat stroke? Take it off!"

She'd been standing on the ragged edge already. Less would have nudged her over.

"With pleasure," she shouted. Her hand flew to her throat and she heard the snarl of her zipper as she yanked it open, wrenched off the jacket, and flung it wrathfully at him. "Damn it, are you happy now?" she yelled tearfully.

Cooler air flooded against her overheated skin, raising prickling sensations as it dried her perspiration. Focused unblinkingly as she was on Neil, she hardly heard the many indrawn breaths, or Alan Despensa's soft, appreciative whistle.

Neil had automatically caught her jacket as his gaze moved from her face to her shoulders, to her bare midriff, and upward to the delicate white lace of her bra that barely concealed the stirring press of her nipples, rapidly hardening under the shock of the rapid temperature change. His eyes returned to her face and never left it as he handed her jacket to Bob Rowen. Laying a hand firmly on the edge of the tablecloth, he gave it one harsh yank that flooded the floor around him with a shower of smashing glassware. He walked through a field of glass splinters and startled onlookers, and came to stand before Kathy. Shaking out the folds of the tablecloth, he draped it with great tenderness around her naked shoulders. Her vision was running like wet watercolors, but through the fog of tears she saw that his face held an odd, gentle expression. The hand that began to stroke slowly over her hair was trembling.

"Darlin', why don't you have a shirt on?" he asked.

"Because," she answered in a thin voice, "someone stole it at the bus station."

"Bus station." He repeated the words blankly, as though he'd never heard of such a place.

"Yes. Bus station. I came by bus, rich boy. How did you think I got here? What are you laughing about?"

Neil's slow, curious smile that had become a husky chuckle was swiftly blossoming into an uncontrollable blend of musical, guileless laughter. "Stratton," she said, "you'd better quit it and tell me just what you think is so darn—" Soft, rather silly whoops wrenched his shoulders as he collapsed against her, his arms spreading around her back to warm her through the linen tablecloth, his face nuzzling like a puppy into the side of her neck. Nudging fiercely against his convulsing chest, she snapped, "What's so funny, you idiot?"

Somehow her words sent him into further showers of laughter. At last he fought for breath. "Darlin', Renee and I—" He stopped, struggling against another outbreak. "Renee and I have the highway patrol in six states looking for you. We thought—we thought—" fresh gales— "you were trying to find your way to California on a moped."

An hour and a half later found Kathy in the serenity of Neil's beautiful villa, fed, showered, and comfortably drowning in one of his soft voile shirts, gazing out a floor-to-ceiling window at the light-spangled hills of Los Angeles. She heard his footsteps returning from the kitchen.

"There probably would have been better places to have acted out that scene than in front of half the Los Angeles press," he said.

Joy whispered through her with the heavy urgency of pain as he fitted his body to her, drawing her back with his hands to receive her full length.

"I don't care." She covered his hands where they lay on her hips. "Do you?"

"Only for your sake," he said, rocking her closer. "You *do* mean to marry me, don't you lady?"

"Yep." The word had a cheerful ring that disguised the intoxicating relief, and arrived with an embarrassing rush of tears. She closed her eyes under the soft, downward stroke of his fingers. They stood for a long time at peace before she felt herself being gently turned. She opened her eyes on his face, dusted in the pollen gold glow of the single distant candle. "Do you know," she murmured, "we haven't had time to kiss?"

"I know," he answered softly, smiling into her eyes. His hands went to the top of her shirt. Slowly his fingers opened each button with loving deliberation. When it was done, he opened his own shirt with one hand, pulling the fabric aside as she came to him. Their flesh touched in a contact as innocent and sweetly eager as the slow meeting of their lips. Tasting, moving against each other in murmurs, their lips strayed lightly over each other's mouths until she felt his breath heat and quicken as he pressed his kiss deeply into her, his arms tightening on her shoulders, shifting her in a slow rotation that rubbed her breasts into and against his body. "I love you," he whispered, drawing her down onto his lap on the yielding surface of a silk pillow. Lifting up one knee, he rested her against it, tucking her shirt back at her sides. One hand came warmly to flatten on her collarbone. The other stroked her cheek with a feather touch. Again, she could feel the slight unsteadiness in his touch.

"Sorry," he said, giving her a rueful grin that told her he was conscious of it also. "Testosterone." He transferred a finger to her ear, tracing the intricate structures with great delicacy. "Two months is a long time."

How typically thoughtful of him to reassure her that there had been no one since her. She gazed at the pale, sparkling eyes and thought in wonder how he loved her lanky, coltish body, and her mediocre voice, and found something remarkable in her perfectly ordinary character.

"I'm glad to think I play havoc with your hormones." She moved her lips against his hand where it lay near her shoulder. Barely touching him with her tongue, she murmured, "Relief is at your fingertips." When she looked back at his face, the firm, erotic lips had relaxed into a smile.

"My desperation to make love to you is exceeded only

by my desperation to talk to you. Darlin', could you marry
an unemployed man?"

"Please?"

He laughed and dragged her close, kissing her hungrily.
"God, I love your little Midwestern speech tricks. I mean
that I want to quit, Kathy. I woke up one morning three
years ago and realized that I hated what I do. It keeps the
kind of people away from me that I want to get close to.
And I hate the ego assault—the artificial highs, the single-
mindedness, the obsession. Do you understand?"

"Yes! But, Neil, I—"

"Honey, wait. Before you say anything, I want to be
sure you know that it's not something I'm doing for you.
You've been the catalyst that's given me the courage to
crawl out of a trap. You see, I couldn't understand at first
what I'd be without the glitter. Is there life after being on
the top? It's all just some kind of an esoteric joke where
you find yourself becoming the sum total of your press
clippings."

"Neil, I understand, I truly do. But you mustn't think—
Neil, your fans really do love you."

"That's the point, Kathy. Why *love?* Why am I displayed
in front of them like some Circus Maximus idol? Whatever
relationship I have with the people who hear my music is
the only part that has any meaning. Why should it be cor-
rupted by hero worship?"

"I guess people like the fantasy of it."

"But Pinocchio wants to be a real boy. I don't want to
be anyone's fantasy. Do you know what I want? A home
with you. In Apple Grove, if you can help me keep warm
in the winter. I want to work on movie scores. In fact, I
already have offers to do two of them."

"You've really started to tell people, then?" she asked
uncertainly. "How did they take it?"

"Better than I thought. To be honest, I can't tell you
what a relief it was. It turned out everyone already suspected. They all seemed to know it was only a matter of
time . . . I'm going to keep writing material for my band as
long as they want me to. And Bobby has a lot of material
of his own they want to try out. Honey, what is it?"

"I guess I had the idea— Well, after you sent me the I
LOVE YOU flowers, when there was nothing for so long . . . Do

you mean you were making plans all that time to be with me?"

He smiled. "Arrogant, wasn't I? The gap after the flowers was because I was heroically trying to give you space. I've always been the aggressor and I know sometimes that robbed you of the chance to have a free choice. I won't do that any more, Kathy. I only did it then because I wanted so badly to make it happen between us."

His fingers barely touched her skin as they played back and forth along the line of her chin and then began lightly to caress her throat. He was right. Two months had been a long time. His smile warmed her like sunshine as she arched backwards in a mute appeal for his hand to ride the aching fullness in her breasts. She watched his eyes fall closed briefly as he brought both hands to her breasts, pressing and cupping them, his thumbs lifting gently at the underside of her nipples.

"Ah, lady," he whispered, "my desperate need to make love to you is starting to overcome—" Words stopped as his mouth found her breast, pressing soft kisses in a circle around the hardening tip, and then catching her nipple with exquisite gentleness between his teeth, stroking it with his tongue, blowing softly over the sensitized surface.

Her voice had taken on a rich pleasured languor as she murmured teasingly, "A hundred and forty dollars, and worth every penny."

"Hmmm?"

"That's what I had to pay to get into your concert tonight. A bus ticket worth a hundred and forty dollars. It was either that or surrender my virtue to a ticket scalper."

"What?"

His head had risen sharply, and she began to laugh at his expression, a surprisingly throaty sound. "Don't look so murderous. You see, he had a customized van—" She stopped, because even in the candlelight she could see that his face had lost color. She remembered he'd just spent three intense days worrying about her. This was too cruel. "It was nothing. Honestly. He didn't try to harm me. Please don't be scared."

"Don't be scared? When I think of the things that could have happened to you . . ."

"Well, don't. I've already had enough of a lecture from

Renee on the phone. You know, your garden looked as though it would be beautiful by moonlight. I think I'll go and take a walk in it until you decide that you want—"

She had begun playfully to rise, but he dragged her back, muffling the rest of her words in his kiss. He cherished her with his mouth and hands, his movements heavy and stirring as he caressed the unclad flesh of her belly and breasts and then lower, moving the flat of his hand over the fabric covering her parted thighs. Lightheaded with desire, she felt him lower her to the floor, opening her jeans as he played gentle kisses over her breasts.

"Neil?" she whispered. "I want children. Do you?"

"Yes. I've been thinking for our first, we could adopt Eric Carpenter."

Suddenly they were both laughing, their lips raining frothy kisses on each other's faces. His lips rested against her chin, his fingers tangled in the soft down as he seared his lips over the long curve of her neck. "Tasting you is paradise," he whispered.

"I don't know, Stratton," she said giddily. The plaintive sigh she meant to produce turned instead into a moan under the deep exploration of his fingers. "I can see what kind of husband you're going to be," she breathed.

"Yes." He lifted his head so their eyes could meet over their sweet, drowsy smiles. "Adoring."

She touched two fingers to his lips. "And adored."

WATCH FOR
6 NEW TITLES EVERY MONTH!

Second Chance at Love ™

____ 06148-4	THE STEELE HEART #52 Jocelyn Day	$1.75
____ 06422-X	UNTAMED DESIRE #53 Beth Brookes	$1.75
____ 06651-6	VENUS RISING #54 Michelle Roland	$1.75
____ 06595-1	SWEET VICTORY #55 Jena Hunt	$1.75
____ 06575-7	TOO NEAR THE SUN #56 Aimée Duvall	$1.75
____ 05625-1	MOURNING BRIDE #57 Lucia Curzon	$1.75
____ 06411-4	THE GOLDEN TOUCH #58 Robin James	$1.75
____ 06596-X	EMBRACED BY DESTINY #59 Simone Hadary	$1.75
____ 06660-5	TORN ASUNDER #60 Ann Cristy	$1.75
____ 06573-0	MIRAGE #61 Margie Michaels	$1.75
____ 06650-8	ON WINGS OF MAGIC #62 Susanna Collins	$1.75
____ 05816-5	DOUBLE DECEPTION #63 Amanda Troy	$1.75

Available at your local bookstore or return this form to:

SECOND CHANCE AT LOVE   Dept. BW
The Berkley/Jove Publishing Group
200 Madison Avenue, New York, New York 10016

Please enclose 75¢ for postage and handling for one book, 25¢ each add'l book ($1.50 max.). No cash, CODs or stamps. Total amount enclosed: $_____ in check or money order.

NAME _____

ADDRESS _____

CITY _____ STATE/ZIP _____

Allow six weeks for delivery.   SK-41